KLICKITAT

KLICK

AMULET BOOKS
NEW YORK

KLICKITAT

PETER ROCK

Library of Congress Cataloging-in-Publication Data
Rock, Peter.
Klickitat / by Peter Rock.
pages cm
Summary: "After Vivian's older sister Audra runs away from home, writing inexplicably appears in a blank notebook. When Audra finally returns in the company of a strange man, the three of them run away together and practice wilderness survival, and Vivian wonders who this mysterious man is." —Provided by publisher.
ISBN 978-1-4197-1894-6 (hardcover) —
ISBN 978-1-61312-897-8 (ebook)
1. Sisters—Fiction. 2. Secrets—Fiction. 3. Survival—Fiction. 4. Mystery and detective stories. I. Title.
PZ7.1.R6395 Kl 2016
2015023958

Printed and bound in U.S.A.
10 9 8 7 6 5 4 3 2 1

Amulet Books are available at special discounts when purchased in quantity for premiums and promotions as well as fundraising or educational use. Special editions can also be created to specification. For details, contact specialsales@abramsbooks.com or the address below.

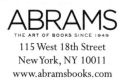

THE ART OF BOOKS SINCE 1949
115 West 18th Street
New York, NY 10011
www.abramsbooks.com

This book is for
Miki Frances & Ida Akiko,
two sisters.

THEY WERE NOT WALKING HAND IN HAND,

BUT THEY FELT AS IF THEY WERE.

—Laura Ingalls Wilder, *The Long Winter*

ONE

It all started when I noticed the way my sister was walking. It was late in the afternoon and I was upstairs in my bedroom, watching her out the window. I'd wedged myself between my bookcase and the wall so they both pressed against me, holding me tight. Below, outside, at the edge of our backyard, I saw Audra.

Her hands were on her knees and she slowly lifted one bare foot, still crouching, then set it down, a small step, and lifted the other. Her body was doubled over so she had to bend her neck back to face ahead, to see where she was going. She was moving very slowly, out from under the trees.

This was not so long ago—a few months ago, when she was seventeen. I was fifteen then and I am sixteen now. Some months can go by and nothing changes, and then everything suddenly becomes different, and all the days get fast and tangled. That's what began when I watched Audra from my window.

She moved slowly around the side of the house, where I couldn't see her. A little later, I heard her voice in the kitchen, downstairs, fighting with our mother. I pushed the bookcase out and went out of my room, down the hall, toward the stairs.

"I'm tired of talking about Thursday," Audra was saying. "That was almost a week ago."

"And you still haven't explained it." Mom was turned away, standing at the sink, peeling potatoes. Five smooth orange carrots were lined up on the counter next to her. "I just don't know when you're telling the truth," she said, "and when you're making things up."

"Why don't you just try believing me," Audra said, "instead of telling me what to do? Also, the way you're shouting is making Vivian upset."

"Are you okay, honey?" Mom said, turning toward me.

"I'm not upset," I said, standing by the kitchen table. "I don't feel agitated."

Audra turned back toward Mom. "And why should I listen to you?"

"Because I'm your mother."

"Right," Audra said. "Of course."

"You don't answer your cell phone. You don't even have it with you, when we paid for you to have it."

"Like I want a machine attached to me all the time," Audra said.

"Is that a tattoo on your arm?"

"No. Someone drew on me with a marker."

"What does it say?" Mom said.

"I can't tell, and I can't remember. A tattoo? Get serious."

Just as Audra held up her arm, showing the blurry blue lines, something from outside struck the window. A terrible, flat sound. The window vibrated and settled and everything became still.

"What was that?" Audra said. "A bird?"

I stepped closer to the window. I could see something moving, through the bushes, on the ground.

"Is it dead?" she said. "Did it break its neck?"

"I don't think so," I said. Now I could see the bird, small and gray, hopping in a kind of circle. It tipped over and flapped its wings against the ground until it could get itself standing up again.

When I turned around, Mom was peeling potatoes, hard, into the sink. She was shorter than Audra, who stood in the middle of the kitchen with her eyes closed and her hands held out in front of her, like she was holding some invisible thing. Audra's hair was dyed black without any shine. Normally it would be the same dirty blond as mine.

Dad's voice called from the basement, then—"What's happening up there?"—but no one answered him.

I noticed how Audra's fingers were trembling a little, as she stood there with her eyes still closed. And then I looked down, out the window again, and I couldn't see where the bird had gone.

"I saw you out there," Mom said. "Whatever you were doing, walking crazy like that. And barefoot, in March."

"You didn't have to watch," Audra said, opening her eyes. "And I can walk however I want—if we always walk the exact same way, we don't see what's around us, we're like robots."

"Robots—I'm tired of hearing that word from you." Mom turned with the peeler in hand, which was not a knife but seemed like a knife. "Are your pants too tight or something, they make you walk like that?"

"What? Jesus, no." Audra's voice rose higher as she unsnapped her camouflage pants, jerked them down. She pulled one leg out and they caught on her other ankle. She almost fell down and then kicked until the pants flew off and hit a kitchen chair. The chair slid into the table, but didn't tip over.

"Audra Hanselman," Mom said.

Audra's legs were pale white and her underwear was yellow. She didn't say anything else, and she didn't pick up her pants. She turned and went up the stairs. I could see the black soles of her feet, going, climbing, and then she was gone. Upstairs, her bedroom door slammed.

"Vivian," Mom said, close to me now. "I was asking if you're all right."

"Fine," I said. "I just need to go outside, to check on something."

"Dinner's in half an hour."

Outside, it was cold, but it wasn't raining. I walked around underneath the window. The bird wasn't there. I looked under the bushes, zigzagged out a little, then started walking around the side of the house, sweeping my eyes back and forth across the ground.

In the front yard there was a rope swing. The black tire hung from a tree branch and the rope was long, so long that Audra could get it going so she swung out over the street and then back again, all the way to the house. High up on the walls of the house, up above the picture window, there were dirty footprints, the marks of where Audra had pushed and kicked off.

The bird was not in the front yard. I looked up, but there were no birds in the sky that I could see. Only the bare branches and then the tall, metal antennas on top of our house. Some kids call it the "Helicopter House" because it looks like the antennas could start to spin and the whole house would lift up. If it did, the basement would still be in the ground, opened up, and looking down into it you'd see my dad's radio outfit, all the wires and lighted dials where red needles lift and jerk back and forth, where voices talk in the thick round padded ears of his headset. You'd see my dad, sitting there, talking to people who live far away.

At first I didn't see Audra, because her hair and her black sweatshirt blended into the shingles. She was sitting there on the rooftop, outside her bedroom window. When she saw me looking up, she didn't say anything. She just slowly lifted her hand and waved. I waved back, then looked away, down again.

I went in the front door, through the living room. Mom and Dad were in the kitchen, talking at the table, and when I picked up Audra's pants from the floor, my parents looked over at me.

"Tell your sister she can stay upstairs until she's ready to apologize," Dad said.

"And bring down your pills, Vivian," Mom said. "So you can take them with your dinner."

Upstairs, Audra's door wasn't locked. I opened it, stepped over the books on the floor, stood next to the open window with the cold air blowing in. Audra turned her head to see who I was. I stared at the left side of her face, with the seven little silver hoops on the edge of her ear.

"I brought your pants," I said, holding them up, but already I could see she'd put on some black jeans.

"It's all right." She didn't turn around. It was quiet for a minute, and then she said, "I didn't expect you to say anything."

"What?" I said.

"Before," she said. "Downstairs. You did the right thing, just watching. I can't help it, and then it's just the same thing, over and over."

"I'm on your side," I said.

"If I can just change the way I do things," she said. "The way I walk and listen and talk and touch—but if I keep trying to change then even that trying starts to be the same, like a rut, a robot trying not to be a robot, and I spend all my time watching myself, you know?"

Now Audra did look around at me, and smiled like I should step through the window and sit on the roof with her. I reached out and felt the grit of the shingles. It felt slippery, like I would slip. I stayed standing where I was.

"I met someone," she said. "Someone who knows all kinds of things, better than the way we're living, here. Closer to how we're supposed to be."

"Who?" I said.

"Soon you'll know," she said. "Everything's going to change."

Two houses down, at the Haydens', a white van that said BEE EXTERMINATOR on it was parked. Across the street, Jimmy Newman was kicking a ball up the hill in his front yard. It was a red ball, and he'd kick it up, and it would roll down, and he'd kick it up again.

I tried to slow down my breathing, but as Audra slid back, closer to me, I felt a trembling start inside me. Strong and too quick for me to get between something and something else, before I could get to my life jacket in my closet in my room across the hall. My arms rose up and my hands were shaking. They reached out and took hold of Audra's arm, of her shoulder where it turned into her neck.

"Vivian," she said, "it's all right. It's fine. I'm here."

And then I could hardly hear her because the blood was roaring around in my body and racing in my ears and all I wanted to do was hold on.

I pulled Audra through the window, onto her bedroom floor, half on top of me next to the bed. She was saying something, over and over again, stroking my hair with her hand that wasn't twisted back under her.

"Klick-i-tat. Klick-i-tat."

That was a game we used to play, when we were younger, that I'd almost forgotten. If we were in trouble, or Mom and Dad were arguing, we'd say that name. "Klickitat," back and forth to each other, to help us feel better, to know that we were always sisters, always together. We got it from Beezus and Ramona, the name of their street—a block away from our street, Siskiyou, here in Portland—and we said it because they are sisters and we are sisters, and because we liked the sound.

"Klickitat," Audra said, whispering, her voice close to my ear. "Klickitat."

It was the word for how we felt together, understanding each other. My fingers began to loosen. A "vise-like grip" is what I've heard it called, where a doctor wrote it in my file, and they've always pried me off people—it's only Audra who let me hold on until it passed, even if the doctors or Mom and Dad tried to pull us apart.

"I'm sorry," I said to Audra.

"It's okay." It was quiet for a moment, and then she said, "Are you getting worse, do you think?"

"I don't know," I said.

"Don't be sorry," she said. "We'll figure out ways to make it better for both of us, for everyone."

Audra sat up, stretched her arms above her head, turned her head from side to side like she was checking to make sure her neck still worked. She smiled at me, and just then Mom started calling that dinner was ready.

Audra did not come down to dinner. Instead, she went back through her window and stayed out all night, later than anyone could stay awake waiting.

TWO

The next morning, Audra still had not come home. I sat at the kitchen table, eating a toaster waffle. A glass of milk, one of orange juice, and my three pill bottles were lined above my plate, all waiting for me. Dad was upstairs, and Mom hurried in and out of the kitchen with a piece of toast in one hand, getting ready to go to work.

"You're buying lunch at school?" she said. "You'll eat something?"

"I'll be okay," I said.

I waited, but she didn't say anything about Audra. She kept talking about work, about being late. My mom works for Nordstrom, where she's a personal shopper.

That means she chooses clothes for people who can't choose their own clothes—either they don't have time or they don't care or they're color-blind or whatever. It also means that she brought home new clothes for us all the time. I used to think this was great until Audra explained that we only got clothes no one else wanted. That no one bought and that were a year old or more. Audra stopped wearing them. She refused. That's one of the things she and Mom fought about, how Audra wore clothes from Goodwill or the Salvation Army.

"Did you take your pills?" Mom said.

"I will," I said.

"I'll count them later."

"Mom," I said.

"Have a great day, honey." She leaned close to kiss the top of my head, and then she went out the door and in a minute I heard her car start and back down the driveway, gone.

Outside, rain was misting down. I squinted up through the window, at the gray sky, and then I stood up, leaned close. On the glass, on the other side of the window, was a faint round mark, and tiny, tiny feathers, stuck there. Right at the spot where the bird had flown into the window. I held up my hand, but my side of the glass was smooth.

Out in the gray morning I could see the trees across the backyard, the small black shapes of birds in the bare branches.

Audra came in only a minute or two later, like she had been watching the house, waiting for Mom to leave. She was wet, and smiling.

"Hey." She picked up the crust of Mom's toast from the plate on the counter and jammed it into her mouth. I could see the wet footprints of her bare feet shining on the linoleum.

"Did you sleep?" I said.

"Of course I slept." Audra poured herself a cup of coffee and walked over close to me. She reached out to touch my arm.

"You smell like a campfire," I said.

"A bonfire," she said, and snorted. "Some idiots were trying to jump their bikes over it. One of them broke his leg, I think."

"Did he get a cast?" I said.

"I don't know," she said. "I left, to go do some other things, to try to find someone."

"Did you?"

Audra didn't answer; she took off her wet coat and hung it up, over the heat vent. She shivered, hugged herself, her wet hair tight and dark around her head. She looked even skinnier than usual, and there was a silver stud in the side of her nose. I knew she wanted me to say something, to notice it.

"Remember that bird that flew into the window?" I said.

"What?"

"Yesterday," I said. "There's still feathers there."

Audra didn't sit down. She just stood there in the middle of the kitchen.

"There's something I want you to do with me," she said.

She reached into the front pocket of her jeans and took out a wrinkled piece of newspaper. I held out my hand, but she didn't give it to me.

"You took your pills, didn't you?" she said.

"Yes," I said, and she gave me a look.

"What?" I said. "I mean, not yet, I haven't."

"They're poisoning you," she said. "So you'll be like them, a robot like everyone else. This house!" Pacing across the kitchen, Audra jerked open the refrigerator, looked into it for a moment.

"I could go with you," I said. "One of these nights."

"You could." Audra looked across the kitchen like she was measuring me. "And you could get hurt. People do."

"You don't," I said. "I wouldn't."

Audra closed the refrigerator. She took a long knife from a drawer, looked at its shining blade, then put it back.

"What was that?" I said.

"The knife?"

"That newspaper in your pocket."

When Audra came back, close to me, her voice was softer.

"It's about the girl," she said. "She lived for four years in the forest, never in a house. Growing things, hiding, reading books. We'll go see her; she'll tell us things."

"When?" I said.

"Soon." Audra folded the newspaper and put it back

in her pocket, then glanced behind her, toward the stairs. "Is Dad still here?"

"I think so."

"I'm taking a shower."

Once she was gone, upstairs, I twisted the tops from my bottles and swallowed my three pills, each a different size and color. Blue, green, yellow. I twisted the lids back on, then drank my milk, then my orange juice.

I took a lot of pills, but no one really understood what was wrong with me. Not the doctors, not my parents, not me. "Becoming agitated" was what they called it, and they wanted me to learn to recognize it, so I could be in control of it and not let it be in control of me.

At school, people gave me space. They flinched sometimes when I came close, or held up an arm like they were going to block me from hitting them. I never hit anyone. The nickname they had for me was "Vivian Ritalin"—but that wasn't even a pill I took anymore. The girls only said things like that when they were in groups and even then they never got too close.

At school I was allowed to carry my backpack with me. In it I kept an old zippered sweatshirt that was too small. If I started feeling like I was becoming agitated, I put it on and zipped it up tight, so it held me and calmed me down.

I was a sophomore, and Audra was a senior. I hardly saw her at school, so she couldn't protect me. The closer she came to graduating, the less often she went to school at all.

It had been easier, we were closer, when we were in different schools. At night, we would sneak across the hallway, sleep in the same bed, whisper all night. She had a black BMX bike with foot pegs, and I'd stand on them, behind her with my hands on her shoulders, and we'd ride through the neighborhood. I could smell her hair. I leaned when she leaned. I saw everything over the top of her head. We would coast along, sisters, and people would see us together, and no one would be moving at the same speed, in the same direction.

THREE

It was a week or so after the bird flew into the window, another one of those nights when Audra went out and didn't come back until the next day. There were new locks on the outside of her bedroom door, on her window, but that didn't stop her.

I was sitting at the desk in my bedroom, doing homework. The window reflected back, it was night, so I could see myself with my social studies book open, my hand taking notes with a pencil. All about Martin Luther King, and how different people should have the same kind of chances, even if they are different. And then I ran out of paper.

In my bookcase, a yellow notebook was caught tight

between my world atlas and an encyclopedia about mammals. It wasn't a new notebook—it had my name on the cover, written by me. By the curliness of my signature, and the color—yellow was my favorite then—I could tell that it was from seventh grade, or eighth. Now, finding it, I pulled the thin white paper snakes from the metal spiral, left behind when the pages were torn out. I balled them up and put them in my pocket.

It had half its paper left, maybe, and I opened the cover. The first page was blank, but I could see writing through it, behind it. I carried the notebook back to the desk and set it down, under the lamp. I opened it again, and turned that first blank page.

The writing was not easy to read. It was not my writing, I didn't know whose it was, and I'd never heard of what the words were saying. The words were cursive. They didn't follow the lines, but slanted across them.

> *There is in fact coming and going, bending*
> *and breaking. One single bolt or screw*
> *holds the blades of a scissors together, into*
> *one tool that can cut paper or leather*

or steel or meat. If you take that screw
or break that bolt, the scissors become
two things. Two knives. Eyes can cut, too,
back and forth. Eyes can turn outward or
inward.

When I read those words, I didn't know the way I was feeling, didn't exactly recognize it. I stood up from my desk and opened my closet and took out my orange life jacket from its hanger. I put it on over my clothes, and hooked the buckles and pulled the straps as tight as I could around me, holding me. Then I slipped down in the space between my bed and the wall, where I could hardly fit with the life jacket on, where I was squeezed and could close my eyes and breathe slowly.

The trembling did not come for me; I was not agitated. It was something else.

I stood up again, walked across my bedroom. I leaned my head against the cold window, so I could see past, through the reflection. Outside, our yard was empty. The shadowy trees blew around in the rain.

I sat down at my desk. I read the words in the notebook again, slower this time. The scissors and the knives, the eyes. And then I turned the page where it had been blank before and now there were more words in that same handwriting, like they'd been written while I was between the bed and the wall.

These words were different, and kind of the same.

A girl is the sweetest, sharpest thing. For how many years are they at their most dangerous? They can drift beyond, and they can home right in. Or is it hone? To hone is to sharpen. To think only of sharpness is a mistake, of course, as girls are also soft, and that is part of their power. Electrical storms become all snarled up in soft clouds. Some of us were once girls, some were never girls. Hello! We're all mixed together now, coming and going, ebbing and flowing, and we do appreciate girls. We need them like a cat with its eyes dialed down to see in a darkness. Have you ever pressed your hand flat to a girl's bare back?

I closed the yellow cover of the notebook and carried it across the hall to Audra's room. I wanted to show it to her. I didn't know yet that she'd gone out, that she'd be gone all night, so I was surprised that her room was empty.

I turned on the light, stepped inside. On the wall above her bed, two hands were outlined, where she'd traced hers in black marker. Waving, or saying "Stay Back." On her bed was a round gray roll of duct tape, a coil of rope.

Audra's favorite books were still there, the ones she always read. *Swiss Family Robinson* and *Kidnapped*, *Treasure Island*, *Journey to the Center of the Earth*, *A Wizard of Earthsea*. And next to them, books I had never seen before. All about surviving in the woods, wilderness medicine, trapping animals with snares. They weren't library books, and they were scuffed, the covers scratched and the titles on the spines impossible to read. I pulled one out, opened it up. The page was smeared with dirt, and one passage was underlined in blue ink:

> *Animals, like humans, make in life*
> *the mistakes that will ultimately*

lead to their death, either physically
or on a spiritual and emotional
level. People and animals that
stay on the same paths in life will
eventually wear themselves into ruts.
Soon the ruts become so deep that
the people can no longer see over
the sides. They see neither danger,
nor beauty, only the path before
them because they fear losing their
security and are afraid to enter the
land of the unknown.

The book was written by a man named Tom Brown, Jr. Farther in, I saw drawings and diagrams of different ways of walking, how to walk without making a sound. The Scout Walk. The Fox Walk.

When I slid the book back among the others, I saw myself, my reflection in the window. I thought how someone outside could see me. Even Audra could see me, as she came home, see me reading her books, standing in her room. I switched off the light, then stepped to the window and looked out. Over our front yard, past the swing, the black street shiny and wet. No one was out there. The only sound was a creak, overhead, as an antenna shifted and turned. That meant Dad was in the basement, trying to find one of his friends, somewhere else in the world.

Light shone from the door of my parents' bedroom, where my mom was sitting at the computer. Their bedroom is at the end of the hall, then mine, then Audra's, across from mine and closest to the stairs.

I went downstairs, into the kitchen, where the light was on, the dinner dishes clean in the drying rack next to the sink. The notebook was still in my hand and I set it on the counter. I poured myself a glass of water and drank it. I took an apple from the refrigerator, but I didn't know if I wanted to eat it. Scissors, cats, lightning, the way girls were powerful and how I was a girl—that was what I was thinking about.

I could hear Dad's voice downstairs, in the basement. He cleared his throat. I heard a hiss as he twisted the cap from one of his two-liter bottles of soda, then the crinkly plastic sound of the bottle as he squeezed it, as he took a drink. I picked up the notebook again and started down, into the basement.

At first he didn't notice me. I sat on the stairs, two or three steps from the bottom, and watched as he turned knobs, as the sharp red needles jerked back and forth in the tiny, lighted windows. His hair had gotten bushy, messy, his beard growing out. He is an accountant, and his work's about counting numbers that are other people's money. Some parts of the year he's really busy, but he spends a lot of time in the basement, talking to people who use names that might not be their real names, people who even used numbers instead of names.

"Vivian," Dad said, turning in his swivel chair, noticing me. "You been there a long time?"

"Not really," I said.

"What's up?" He looked worried, kicking with his feet to roll closer to me. Instead of shoes, he wore the ragged gray felt liners from winter boots. He also wore his old ski jacket, with stripes down the arms and holes in the front, where one time he'd carried a car battery.

Now he pulled the headset down, around his neck.

"Everything all right? Nothing's wrong, bothering you, is there?"

"Not really," I said, and then I realized that I was still wearing the orange life jacket, that's what he was looking at. I loosened the straps, smiled back at him. I shifted the notebook behind me; perhaps I had been going to show it to Dad, but suddenly in that moment I knew that I did not want to share it, that I wasn't supposed to.

"Who are you talking to?" I said.

"Some people," he said. "A lady in Iceland I know, a new person in Thailand."

"What are you talking about?"

"The weather, mostly. I mean, just talking. They're pretty lonely, I guess. Sometimes I just listen to conversations other people are having."

"Without them knowing?" I said. "Is that okay?"

"Yes," he said. "That's how it works. They can listen in on me, if they want to."

Sitting there, watching as my dad put his headset back on, as he flipped switches and turned dials, I think then I understood how lonely, or how dissatisfied, he was—how he was trying to reach, to talk to people who were not in our house, not in our family. And upstairs, my mom was at her computer, looking somewhere else, too. Audra had always talked to me, and I had talked to her, but now even Audra had someone else, somewhere else, this person who knew more than I did, this girl who knew things, who knew how to live out in the woods.

Dad turned around; he lifted the headset from one ear. "What are Audra and your mom up to?"

"Nothing," I said. "Mom's in the bedroom with the computer, I think. Audra, I don't know. I should do my homework."

"Good girl," he said.

I turned and climbed back up into the kitchen, through it and up the stairs toward my bedroom. At the top, outside Audra's door, is where the floor creaks. If you know how to step there, your feet wide, right where the floor meets the wall, you can still do it silently.

Back in my room, I took off my life jacket, hung it in the closet, then set the yellow notebook on my desk. I opened it, read through those words again.

To think only of sharpness is a mistake,
of course, as girls are also soft, and that
is part of their power. Electrical storms
become all snarled up in soft clouds.

That was about me. I liked that these words were being sent to me, only for me. I was a girl with a snarl inside. A snarl is a knot, a tangle, and it can also be a sound.

FOUR

I waited until lunchtime. Then I walked right across the sports fields, past groups of kids who were talking on their cell phones, not paying attention to anything around them. Still, I kept expecting someone to call out or come after me. I didn't turn back to look at the windows of the school where some teacher might be watching, wondering where I was going.

And once I was out of sight, turning the corner and down the street, Audra was standing there, right where she said she'd be. She just looked up and waited, and then we walked along without saying anything, past the QFC supermarket, past Beverly Cleary Elementary, down toward the highway and the MAX train station. I looked back, once. No one was following.

We crossed a parking lot, then the bridge above the train tracks. We could already hear the train coming, so we ran down the stairs to the platform.

On the train we swung our backpacks around and set them on the floor. Audra smiled at me, reached out and touched my shoulder. There was ink all over her right hand, the words too smeared to read. She is left-handed.

"This girl knows a lot," Audra said. "She taught herself with books instead of going to school, grew her own food. She was hiding all the time, invisible—no one could find her."

"So we're going to the woods?"

"No," Audra said. "They caught her, finally, moved her to another place, said she had to go to school."

"You said no one could catch her."

"It was an accident, getting caught. It wasn't her fault. Still, there's a lot of things she can teach us."

The ring where Audra's nose had been pierced was gone. Her ears were covered by her hair swinging down, but her hair wasn't snagging on her earrings like it usually did.

"Like what?" I said.

"What?" Audra said.

"What's she going to teach us? How to be like her?"

"No," Audra said. "How to be like ourselves."

"Okay," I said, not sure what she meant. I felt the wheels clacking through the floor, through the soles of my sneakers. The train went around a curve, the middle part bending like an accordion.

"I mean, what do you think's going to happen to me?" Audra said. "I'm supposed to go to college, then meet some guy and probably marry him and then every day we both wake up and drive to work where we sit in cubicles and there probably aren't even any windows or anything?"

Her voice was loud enough that people were looking over at us. I unzipped my pack and touched my too-small sweatshirt, but then I looked at Audra and the feeling passed.

"*That's* pretending to be a different person than who you are," she said.

"What are you talking about?" I said.

"There's nothing worse than living that way," she said. "Like your life jacket, or that sweatshirt—do you think you'd need that, really, if you stopped taking those pills they make you swallow?"

"I don't know what I'd do," I said.

"But sometimes it still happens—like you still grab me, even when you've taken the pills, right? So maybe you don't need the pills at all."

"If I didn't take them," I said, "Mom and Dad would know. Mom counts them every night."

The train was starting over the river, across the bridge. Down below, there were only a couple of small boats. It wasn't raining, but it looked like it could start.

"Whatever," Audra said. "Just think about how you feel—just feel how it all is. It doesn't make sense the way it is, or the way it's been. I mean, Mom and Dad? Do we want to end up like them, all boring and sad? In front of a computer or a radio? Attached to a cell phone?"

The train slid into Pioneer Square, the center of Portland. Groups of kids stood out there, close together, kicking hacky-sacks, smoking. One got on the train, his short hair yellow, a dirty Band-Aid on his cheek. His black pants had straps and buckles all over them, and he'd brought his bicycle, a really tiny one, onto the train. He stood there as the doors slid closed and then Audra got up and walked over to him. They were talking, but I couldn't hear them. She asked him a question; he shook his head. She pointed at his bike; he pointed up in the air, down at the floor. He looked at her and smiled.

Audra turned and came back and sat next to me just as the train went into the tunnel. I could see us both in the black window, how our faces looked kind of the same. Audra's was sharper, the shadows darker in her eyes.

"You know that guy?" I said.

"Not really," she said.

"What were you talking about?"

"He said he's going to race that little bike all the way down the hills from the zoo, back to Pioneer Square. Some friend of his is timing him on a watch."

"Why aren't they in school?" I said, but Audra didn't answer.

The train slid to a stop at the underground station beneath the zoo. It was lit like a cave, and the boy got off. We could see him standing at the elevator, spinning the bike on its front wheel, holding the handlebars, and then he stepped into the elevator and the doors closed behind him.

Out of the tunnel, in the day again, the train climbed farther away from the city.

"Where are we going?" I said. "Beaverton?"

"Next stop we get off," Audra said. "We transfer over to a bus."

We had to wait near a parking lot, near Best Buy and Walmart and Home Depot, before the bus came. We picked up our packs and climbed on.

"It's not too much farther, I think," Audra said. "It's just outside of town."

Reaching over, I put my hand in her hand, her fingers dry and rough.

"Are you afraid?" she said.

"No."

"It's all right to be afraid," she said. "You should be, actually."

"Does the girl know we're coming?" I said. "Won't she be in school?"

"We'll see," she said. "We'll wait for her. You know, she's closer to your age than mine, but she knows so much."

"I know things," I said.

Audra laughed, then looked away, out the window. An old lady was pushing a shopping cart. The wind blew her hat off her head and it was hard for her to bend down and pick it up.

"So now this girl lives in a house?" I said.

People were getting on and off the bus, pulling the cord to ring the bell, pushing their way down the aisle. I was thinking of all that Audra had said, how she'd been, lately. I tried to guess what she was going to do—it had something to do with this girl, and living in a way that wasn't our parents' way. Our parents had told Audra that once she graduated from high school she could live at home only if she got a job or registered at Portland State, for college. I didn't think she was going to take either of those choices.

Out the window, strips of pale blue showed between the clouds, sliding quickly through the sky. I tried to pull my hand back from Audra, but she held tight and I stopped pulling.

The closer we got to the girl, the less eager I was to arrive, to meet her. Was I jealous? Audra had changed so much, had moved so much further away from me since she met her. The books in Audra's room, I realized, they belonged to the girl. It was like Audra wanted another sister, a girl who knew all about the wilderness and how to live inside it. Those were things I did not know.

FIVE

The bus kept going, taking us out of the city. There were fields, and barbed-wire fences, and groups of cows and horses out in the fields. I watched, feeling Audra next to me and not wanting to share her. I tried to imagine how it would feel if there were three of us.

"Here." Audra pulled the cord that rang the bell and the bus slowed down. "We're getting off here."

We walked on the side of the road, the dirty gravel. Audra took off her black Chuck Taylors; she tied the laces together and put them around her neck, her socks pushed inside.

"Is that the Fox Walk?" I said.

"You know," she said, "people never wore shoes until there were roads and sidewalks."

"What are we doing with this girl?" I said. "What do you have planned?"

She didn't answer, like she didn't hear me.

"Audra," I said. "What are we going to do?"

"I don't know that, yet." She walked so balanced, like the sharp rocks didn't hurt her. She was always the fastest person in her class, even faster than the boys. When she got to high school she stopped running. She said it was boring, that it was showing off.

After a little while we came to a yellow house with a peeling fence in front. The house had cardboard in one window. One of the rain gutters was broken and hanging down toward the ground. A dog started barking.

"Chainsaw!" a boy said, coming out the front door.

Another boy with the same white blond hair was behind him. The dog was still barking, running along the other side of the fence like it was trying to find a place to get through, to get at us.

"She's old," the boy said. "She can't hear anything

at all." Now he had a hold of the dog's collar, and was watching us. "Who are you?" he said.

"Travelers," Audra said.

The boy was maybe ten or eleven. His brother was younger, and wasn't wearing a shirt.

"She's friendly," the first boy said. "Don't worry."

"We're not," I said.

"Where are you guys going?" the boy said, but we were already walking away, farther down the road.

Horses came toward us, following along the fence line, on the other side. Their long necks stretched over, with white stripes down their faces. Behind them were cows, and I couldn't tell if they were all separated by a fence or if the cows just stayed with the cows and the horses with the horses.

"Everything will be fine," Audra said.

"I didn't say anything," I said.

We came to a gate where there was a dented gray mailbox on top of a post. Gold stickers on the mailbox said 323.

"Here we are," Audra said.

She opened the mailbox; it was empty; she slapped

it shut. I followed her through the gate, up a long gravel driveway, toward a tall house. We passed two red barns, and a smaller building, down a slope from the house. When we got to the house, we climbed up on the wooden porch. Audra's feet made almost no sound on the porch. Mine in their sneakers did.

"Is she here?" I said.

Audra knocked on the door, and we waited. It was quiet, and I leaned close to a window so I could see inside. A grandfather clock, a stack of books that looked like it was about to tip over. Hanging on a wall was something that might have been a trap for a bear.

"Hello!" A man suddenly came around the side of the house, out around the porch, behind us. "What can I do for you?"

He just stood there, squinting up at us. He was kind of old, his head shiny bald. He wore red suspenders, and also a belt.

"We're friends of the girl," Audra said. "Is she here?"

"The girl?" he said.

"Caroline," she said. "She's a friend of ours, from school, we came to visit her. Maybe she's not home yet?"

"I think you don't understand," he said. "Listen—"

"Does she live in that little house down there?" Audra pointed.

"You're barefoot," he said.

"I know that," she said. "Her name is Caroline. Is Caroline here?"

The man stepped a little closer and put out a hand so he could lean on the railing of the porch. He wore yellow felt gloves and licked his lips before he said anything.

"Yes," he said. "She lived down there, with her father. But that was last summer. That was months ago."

"Where is she now?" Audra said.

"I'd be interested to know that myself," he said. "It seems like you've seen her, if she's your friend. You see her at school?"

"Why did she leave?" Audra said. "What did you do?"

"What did *I* do? I did a lot for them, everything I could. I wanted to help, but they were suspicious people. Her father, he just got a little paranoid, you know? He was used to another way of living."

Now the man stepped closer to us, and we both stepped backward. He opened the door and looked at us like we might want to follow him, come inside.

"Sorry I can't help you." The man nodded and stepped into his house, then closed the door.

"Liar," Audra said, low so he couldn't hear it, the door already closed. Then she touched my shoulder and we went down the steps off the porch.

"You said you knew her," I said.

"I never said that," she said. "Quiet. Stay close to me."

We hurried down the slope, toward a line of old tractors and cars, vehicles that had no tires, not even wheels, that had long grass growing up through them. Audra had a hold of my arm and pulled me back between them, staying low.

"What are we doing?" I said.

Audra tucked her hair behind her ear, and her ear was bare, just the row of dimples where the holes were, where the studs and rings usually were. I looked at the side of her face and noticed, then, that she wasn't wearing the black eyeliner she usually did, that Mom said made her look like a raccoon. Today her brown eyes looked plain and clear, not angry.

"You look pretty," I said.

"Get ready." Audra had her finger to her lips. She peeked over the top of the car. "When I go, you follow me close. Stay low. Do what I do."

Then we were out in the open again, rushing through the ragged grass, up to the door of the smaller house, at the bottom of the slope. There was a lock on the door but Audra did something with her hands and the lock came off. She set it carefully down on the wooden stairs and then pushed the door open.

When we stepped inside it was colder, even quieter than it was outside. She closed the door behind us and we just stood there for a moment.

There was a stove, a picnic table, a refrigerator with its plug pulled out and its cord on the floor. I heard a scratching in the ceiling, mice up there. A poster on the wall showed the planet Earth, floating in space, all the oceans and the continents, America and Oregon, all the cities and forests, all the people invisible, too small to see.

"This is where she was," Audra said.

"What if he finds us in here?" I said. "That man."

We were whispering, but still our voices echoed, a little.

"I don't know," she said. "What's he really going to do? He probably wouldn't even care. Here, this way . . ."

We went through the room and it was so dusty I could see Audra's bare footprints on the wooden floor. Through a door, through a narrow room with one single bed in it, then into another bedroom that was a little bigger.

"This is her room," Audra said, her arms out wide. "Can you feel it?" She began to pull out the drawers of a dresser. They were all empty.

The room had one window and through it I could see part of a rust-colored horse. It was rubbing its long neck along the side of an old outhouse. Standing there, watching Audra, I was so happy, so relieved that the girl was gone, that she wasn't there. It was only the two of us, whatever we were doing.

"It's different, if she lived with her dad," I said. "She had help, I mean. You said she lived by herself, all those years."

"What?" Audra got down on her hands and knees, looking for something.

"You said you knew her. That she told you things—"

"I did not say that," she said. "Vivian—"

"You said you met someone," I said. "Someone different than everyone else."

Audra whirled on me, still on her knees, her voice breaking from its whisper: "That wasn't her. That was someone else. Someone very important."

"Who?" I said.

"He's gone," she said, her voice soft again. "He went somewhere for a little while. I'm waiting for him to come back. I thought, while he's gone, I could still prepare. That's why we need to talk to the girl, so when he comes back he'll know I'm learning things, that I'm the one."

Audra got down on her hands and knees, her ear to the floor, peeking under the bed. Then she reached out and I saw it, a long, dark-colored hair snagged on a rough part of the wooden wall. She held it up in the light and we both looked at it, without having to say that it was hers, the girl's. Audra wound it around and around her finger, into a tiny coil, so small, and put it in the breast pocket of her shirt. She buttoned the pocket.

The bed was covered by a stained wool blanket, and next Audra pulled that back and underneath was only a bare striped mattress with its buttons worn down so the metal showed. She pushed at the edge of the mattress with her knee, lifted up the edge. A piece of paper fell out, down onto the floor.

After she read it, she handed it to me:

> A conversation is a spoken
> exchange of thoughts, opinions
> and feelings. A feeling is a
> tender emotion. An emotion is
> a state of mental agitation or
> disturbance, a feeling.
> Caroline
> Caroline
> Caroline

I handed the scrap of paper back to Audra, but later at home I asked and she let me keep it. I compared it to the writing in my yellow notebook, but it wasn't close to the same. The girl's writing was even and perfect. Every *a* was the same as every other *a*, every *t* like every other *t*.

"Are you feeling okay?" Audra said, that day when we

went to see the girl who wasn't there. We were about to run back out of that little house, across the field, past the empty mailbox, back toward the bus and home.

"I think so," I said.

"I love you, Vivian," Audra said. "You know that, right? I'll always take care of you. No one else knows how."

SIX

Even though I was relieved that we didn't find the girl, I still worried. I couldn't guess what Audra was planning to do, and she wouldn't tell me anything.

I kept thinking that I would show her the words in the yellow notebook, the messages that had come to me, only me. But I also didn't want to share them. If I told someone else, the words might stop coming. I think I was also saving the secret of those messages, in case I needed it, to show Audra that I knew things, too, that I should not be left behind.

I started to worry that the words in the yellow note-book might fade away, or disappear, so I began to copy them into another notebook. That's how I began to write

this all down, so I wouldn't lose anything. And the afternoon I started copying it, sitting at my desk in my room,
I found new writing, a blank page that wasn't blank anymore.

The sea is a flat stone without any
scratches, a fairy tale is a made-up story,
history is a story of the before, and even a
made-up story is made up of real things.
Does static really mean stillness, a lack
of motion? We never stop moving, we are
always here, listening; still here and yet far
from still. Different worlds are all around
us, some easier to see, some too distant,
too far beyond. Hello, we are interested in
you. You're a nice smooth girl, a person.
Girls slip and shift; they disappear, they
can become another person. People band
together for protection or they don't even
know why, and we think it's the tenderest
thing when members of different species
befriend one another. A kitten and a

monkey, a duck and a cow, a dog and a
chicken. We find this so surprising, and feel
that it demonstrates something important
about kindness, and how natural it is when
we let it happen.

Even though the writing was cursive, every now and then a letter didn't fit, like a capital *A* in the middle of a word. It was ragged, the words sometimes stretched out, sometimes crushed together. It was like no one's handwriting I'd ever seen, and the paper was smudged, dirt rubbed into it from the hand dragging along, writing the letters. I wondered whose hand that was, who wrote those words—yet even then I could feel that the messages came from somewhere else, beyond the places and people I knew, to find their way to me. Only to me. And it was true that since I'd received the messages I hadn't felt so agitated, hadn't felt the agitation come over me. The messages were confusing and calming at the same time.

I sat there, copying the new words. It was late in the afternoon; I looked up at my bookcase, to check if there were other forgotten notebooks, but there were only my encyclopedias, my books about animals.

Next to my newer books were books that were passed down from Audra, which were too young for me. I had no one to pass them down to, so they stayed in my room. *The Boxcar Children* and *Island of the Blue Dolphins* and *Beezus and Ramona*—we'd gone to Beverly Cleary Elementary, and in the park near our house there were statues, one of Henry Huggins and his dog, Ribsy, one of Ramona. Audra and I used to play Beezus and Ramona; I stopped liking that game when Ramona started seeming like a brat to me. And then we'd play *Little House on the Prairie*—I was Laura and Audra was Mary, and I described everything to her because she went blind. I led her through the house, blindfolded, all around the neighborhood, and she held on to my arm, unable to see, unable to do the simplest thing without my help.

Looking at my shelves, thinking of Audra, made me miss her, made me want to talk to her. I finished my copying, hid the yellow notebook in the bookshelf, then stood and crossed the hall.

I pushed her door open. The empty room smelled

damp, like wet clothes and dirt, and it felt quieter, the air a soft hiss in my ears. There was a new lock on the window, though by that time I think they'd given up on the locks because she always found a way out. Above her bed, where her hands had been outlined in black marker, there was now another pair of hands, a little higher. Larger hands.

I stood for a moment in the doorway, not going in, and then I felt Mom, behind me, in my parents' room. I turned, but she didn't see me. She was sitting at the computer desk, her side to me, and her face was glowing red from the computer screen, then orange, then blue as the pattern changed. Her mouth moved, but made no sounds. She wore headphones over her ears, and her hair was pulled back tight with a rubber band, which made her head look smaller, her eyes squinted down.

She was barefoot, too, sitting at the computer. All the colors on the screen burst and twisted and unfolded from each other so slowly. Circles and swooping curves, and she sat perfectly still and stared into them, her eyes half-closed.

These are visualizers, these things she does. I knew

that if I talked to her she probably wouldn't hear me, or maybe she was ignoring me. I knew in her headphones there was soft music with no voices, so soft that it's hardly music at all. Mom had tried to get me to do it. She said it was a meditation, refreshing like sleep only even better than sleep. She also has a light shaped like a triangle that is supposed to shift her rhythms, to help her sleep, that she sometimes sets next to her at the dinner table. It tries to convince her body that the sun hasn't gone down.

"Vivian!" she suddenly said, not quite turning around. She'd seen me in the reflection of the screen. "That's creepy, sneaking up on me."

"I was just standing here."

Now her headphones were off, she was facing me. I could tell she was trying not to be angry. Behind her, blue spirals bounced against each other, around the screen.

"It's okay," she said. "Here."

I stepped closer to her, where she was holding out her arms, but we didn't touch. She knew it wasn't always easy for me to touch people.

"We have to try and help each other," she said. "To

be a family. With your sister the way she is right now and everything—"

"Okay," I said.

"We're more than some random people put together in a house."

"I know," I said, feeling awkward, standing there. "It's not your fault."

"What's not my fault?" she said.

"How things are," I said. "With Audra, with me."

Turning, I tried to walk like a fox, silent on the edges of my feet as I went back into the hallway, down the stairs, and through the kitchen.

Downstairs, all the little glass squares of Dad's radio were dark, the red needles still. There's enough light from the windows up by the ceiling, along the driveway. I sat in Dad's rolling swivel chair, the seat patched with tape. Behind me in the darkness, the washer and dryer sat, silent. A pad of paper hung on a hook, but it just had numbers and times listed on it, no real writing. I found another notepad wedged behind a box on the desk, and I took it out and leaned close, squinting to read it—

Iceland is talking about the Number
Stations again. She says the volcano
can block radio waves but that her
transmitter is mobile. She's using the
Earth-Moon-Earth technique, bouncing
her signal off the Moon and down to
me. Imagine her voice, traveling all
that way through outer space and
all that static to reach me. It's so
surprising how people are brought
together, and which ones.

Dad's handwriting is printing, kind of like you learn
in school, only smaller, neater. If you looked at his writing from across the room you might think it was lines of
numbers.

I took the headset from its hook and fit the padded
black foam over my ears. I could hear nothing, only a
faint rushing. The dials were here, the switches. I had
watched Dad do it so many times that I knew I could turn
it all on, line up the numbers. I had talked to people far
away before, heard their tiny voices say hello in my ears.

I felt it then, a change in the house. I was nervous, I couldn't hear, and I put the headset back and stood up, and waited.

"Vivian!" Audra shouted. "Are you home? Where are you?"

"Here," I said, already upstairs, halfway into the kitchen.

She was all the way on the second floor, waiting for me at the top of the stairs.

"Were you in my room?" she said.

I didn't say anything.

"I know someone was," she said. "I put a piece of spiderweb on my door, across the top, and it's broken. So I know someone was in there. Mom's home?"

I looked across the hall; the door to our parents' room was closed.

"It was me," I said. "I pushed it open because I missed you."

"Oh," she said. "That's good. That it was you, I mean. Not Mom and Dad again. They're always saying they respect my privacy, but they're into everything, all the time. Here, come in, talk to me while I get ready."

I climbed the stairs and walked by close to her, close enough to smell her sweat, her hair. I sat on her bed.

"Girls?" Mom said, coming down the hallway.

Audra closed the door so we couldn't hear the rest of what she was saying. I could feel Mom, standing there for a moment, then heard her turn and walk back down the hall.

"What are you getting ready for?" I said.

She pulled down the ragged tights she was wearing, kicked them into the closet, and started pulling on her camouflage pants.

"You're not wearing underwear?" I said.

She opened a drawer of her dresser and took something out, held it up. It was white, thin ropes wrapped tightly around themselves.

"I'm going to sleep in the trees," she said. "High up in the branches, in Mount Tabor Park."

"What?" I said.

"It's a hammock," she said. "No one will know where I am."

"Can I come?" I said.

"Not this time." Audra was opening and closing drawers, looking up to check on me. "You know," she said, "you can come in here anytime, look at anything you want."

"Are you running away?" I said.

Audra laughed. "That sounds so stupid, if you say it like that, like a little kid who's rebelling."

"Are you?"

"Rebelling?"

"No," I said. "Running away."

"I'm going somewhere," she said. "That's different."

"Where?" I said.

Audra didn't say anything at first. She just looked around at the walls of her room like she hated them.

"People aren't supposed to live in cities," she said. "It's so claustrophobic. And we live in a suburb, which is even worse—every person in our neighborhood is exactly the same."

"Not exactly," I said.

"Vivian," she said. "You know what I mean."

The back of Audra's hair was clumping together, not

quite like dreadlocks, and the bones in her face seemed sharper. She was starting to look kind of like another person, a woman, not like a girl anymore.

"Whose hands are those?" I said.

"Where?"

"On the wall. The bigger ones."

"A friend," she said, and didn't say anything more, turning away, filling up her pockets with things I couldn't see.

"Did he come back?" I said. "The one who disappeared?"

"Yes," she said. "He came back for me."

"Where's he from?" I said.

"Not the city," she said. "A long ways from here. That's where we're going."

"When?" I said. "Just you and him?"

Audra glanced out the window, where the shadowy trees were swaying, then checked the hammock, all folded up in her hand.

"Don't worry," she said to me, and then she went around me, out of the bedroom, down the stairs.

In a moment I heard the front door open, slam shut,

and then I saw her walking away, pushing the tire so it swung up, loose on its rope, back and forth behind her as she went down the street.

That was the night when Audra waited until we were all asleep and then she broke the screen of the television in the living room, shattered it so it looked like a spiderweb. She somehow took the computer in my parents' room apart, too, unscrewing the plastic cover and taking pieces out so it would never work again.

She did this all silently, while Mom and Dad were asleep in their bed. That was one reason she'd studied all those ways of walking, to do things like that.

SEVEN

It took a day or two to know that Audra was really gone. It felt different, the house felt different, the three of us wondering and worrying in different ways, trying to understand what was happening.

On the third day I stood in a thin beam of sunlight, next to the window the bird had crashed into. The window was clear, the bird's feathers washed away.

I started down the stairs, peeking through the railing. It was dark down there except for the lights in the tiny windows of the radio. Dad had the headset on and he was slumped over, his elbows on the desk and his hands over his face.

I got close so I could hear sounds and voices buzzing in the air, nothing I could understand. And when I came around the side of him I saw that his eyes were closed. He jumped a little when I reached out and touched his shoulder, then opened his eyes and looked at me.

"Are you feeling okay?" he said, his voice louder than it had to be. He pulled the headset down around his neck, reached to switch off the radio.

I turned and went up the stairs, not stopping when he called my name. I should have told him not to worry, but I didn't. I should have told him that Audra was fine, wherever she was. She was out there, somewhere—I felt it, even though it would be days before I found the note she'd left in my underwear drawer. It was wrapped with twine around a heavy pocketknife, a folding knife with just one sharp blade that I still have, and a magnifying glass. The note said: *The most important rule, then, for anyone who is suddenly faced with a survival situation, is to keep from panicking.*

I knew that, of course. I wasn't going to panic, but still I was confused and unhappy to be left behind.

Ten times a day I checked my notebook to see if there were new words for me. In those first days without Audra, the pages were blank. I took out a pen and wrote, as small as I could, at the top of the next blank page: **Where is my sister? What do you want me to do?**

Those first days, Mom and Dad worried about me, too. They gave me Audra's cell phone, the one she'd left behind, and kept asking me if anyone had called it. The only calls I got were from them, Mom and Dad, checking that I was okay and wanting to know where I was.

I think they wondered why I wasn't more upset, and they thought I knew something, that Audra had told me something that she hadn't told them. They kept asking and asking and I said I didn't know. Then they stopped asking, like that would make me want to come and tell them what I knew.

Mom talked about how Audra had been hanging out with new people, people we didn't know. She said someone could have taken Audra, that anything could have happened.

This was at dinner, and I sat there between Mom

and Dad with Audra's chair empty. Mom's pyramid light, next to her, made one side of her face bright and the other all shadowy. Dad had set out an extra plate and a fork and a knife, like that might bring my sister back at any moment, like she'd sit down to eat the chicken casserole with us.

"I feel so hopeless," Mom said, then.

Dad reached out and touched my arm. "How are you feeling, Vivian?"

"I don't know," I said.

"What about the kids at school?" Mom said.

"What about them?"

"Do you think they know anything?" she said. "Is anyone saying anything?"

"About Audra?" I said. "They wouldn't. We don't talk to the same people. No one really talks to me."

Audra's white plate reflected the lamp in the ceiling. The room was too quiet and it was dark outside and the windows were like mirrors showing the three of us to ourselves. I felt awkward, bad for Mom and Dad, but right then we couldn't help each other. Sitting there, I could see straight through the doorway, into the living room where the television still sat with its screen shattered in a web.

"We can't really make her do anything," Dad said. "We know that. She has to want to come back."

"*If* she can come back," Mom said.

"We have to assume she's all right," he said.

"We do?" she said.

"*I* have to," he said.

"It's just that she left all her things," Mom said. "Where could she have gone without her things?"

I'd already searched around Audra's room, just as my parents had, looking for clues. There were no answers really, no notes or plans or letters or maps left behind. Just all the clothes Mom gave her from Nordstrom that she never wore, all her schoolbooks, her running trophies with the plastic, golden girls on top. The handprints on the wall.

What I didn't tell them was that the books were missing. It was hard to see that because the shelf was a mess and there were still so many books on it, but some of her favorites and all the survival books were missing, taken wherever she'd gone, where she'd need them.

I didn't know, I couldn't believe that she was already gone for good, far away from our city like she'd said. I wrote her a note and left it folded in her desk drawer:

Here I am. I am not panicking.
Klickitat. I know that you would
not truly leave me behind.

EIGHT

The next morning, I slept late. The house was quiet when I woke up. I couldn't hear anyone moving around.

I got dressed and put my books in my backpack, and that's when I saw it. My phone, the cell phone that had been Audra's, was on my desk, all shattered. Not just the screen part—the whole thing was broken into pieces, so the plastic numbers and the battery and the wires were all loose, spread out so there was no way it would ever work again.

Audra had come in the night, had stood so close and hadn't awakened me. I went into her room, which looked the same, even though it felt different. Maybe I was just getting used to her being gone, being in her room alone, but still I thought or wanted to think that she might be coming back in the night, picking up things she'd need, checking on me while I slept.

Out the window I could see the tree, the swing, a blue car driving past.

I looked at the handprints on the wall, her bed made more neatly than she would ever make it, the Nordstrom dresses hanging in her open closet.

I was afraid to check her drawer, to be disappointed; when I looked, though, the note was gone. That meant that Audra had not left me behind, that she could not be too far away.

Next, I went downstairs, past the kitchen table with my plate and cereal bowl and pill bottles where Mom had set them. As I began to sit down, I heard static, like wind in the basement, a hissing, then a beeping.

"Dad?" I said.

There was no answer.

Downstairs, I could see the needles, jerking in the lit windows, and hear the hiss coming from the headset where it hung on its hook. I fit it over my head, over my ears. I listened, the static thick and then quieter, the channels lining up, somewhere out in the air, and some-one surfacing.

"TF8GX calling N7NTU. CQ, TF8GX."

N7NTU is Dad's call sign. On the radio, when you say "CQ" that means "Seek You"—you're letting some-one know you're trying to reach them. Sometimes you arrange a time when you'll be on a certain frequency, and other times you just hope they're there.

"Hello?" I said. "Hello?"

"Be happy, Oregon," a voice said. "This is Iceland."

The voice had an accent; I'd never heard one like it before. Maybe that was partly the radio, the distance. And the voice sounded like a boy, maybe, but more like a woman. Dad had said Iceland was a woman, a friend of his.

"It's not him," I said. "I'm his daughter."

"He's looking for you. Have you returned?"

"No," I said. "That's not me. I'm the younger one."

"Vivian," Iceland said. "Yes, of course. I have been hearing about you for a long time. I know a lot about you."

"Like what?" I said.

"And now we're having a conversation." Static pushed into her voice, then back away. "Has your sister returned?"

"No," I said.

"I lost my sister, too," she said. "Five years ago. Berglind was her name."

I glanced over at the washer and dryer, up at the small window by the ceiling, a piece of gray sky. It was hard to turn my head, the headset's cord against my neck.

"How is your father doing with all this?" Iceland said. "With your sister gone?"

"All right," I said. "Okay, I guess."

"It must have been a surprise," she said.

"I guess so," I said. "I don't know."

"It's so cold and beautiful here, now," she said.

"Are you really in Iceland?" I said. "Or is that just a name you use?"

"The sea looks like metal and the sky is clear. I was out hunting eiderdown this morning, on the lava flows, the nests there. It grew so windy and I'm so old and not steady. I have to use two canes, to walk on the flows."

"How old are you?" I said.

"When I was a girl," she said, static creeping into her words, "I couldn't walk at all. I just sat in a wheelchair and watched the barges go by. I would daydream about all the places they'd go, all the places I could not go. How is your weather?"

Then the static rose and tangled; I thought I could still hear her, pieces of words in that snarl, then I thought I lost her. I was about to take off the headset when things cleared again.

"The static," I said.

"Some think it's only noise," she said. "That is incorrect. Sometimes it's interference from lightning, or in the atmosphere. Sometimes it's simply too many people trying to talk at once, trying to reach you."

"Trying to reach me?" I shivered, the headset's cord sliding across my bare neck.

"So many signals," she said. "All at once. Some say static is the lack of motion, but that is incorrect. Static means there is so much movement in so many directions that the vibration is inward, not outward."

"Like on a television screen," I said. "That kind of static."

"Did you answer me," she said, "before, about your weather?"

"It's raining here," I said. "I haven't been outside yet today, though."

"Do you think," she said, "do you think that people are really talking about weather when they talk about weather, or are they talking about something else?"

"Like what?"

"Like how they are actually feeling."

"I don't know," I said. "Weather, I guess."

"You must miss your sister," she said. "I certainly miss mine—though I still talk to her on the radio."

"How?" I said. "You said she was lost."

"Berglind died, yes," she said. "But sisters have all sorts of ways to find each other. You are a special girl. Your Audra will come back, somehow."

"She's not dead," I said.

"Did I say she was? Good-bye, Vivian. Perhaps we'll speak again. Look after your father, now."

I sat there for a moment in Dad's rolling office chair. His old jacket was on the back of the chair and I pulled it over my shoulders. I put my bare feet in his scratchy gray boot liners. And then I opened the logbook and looked at it. On one side were some sentences—**Audra, gone 3/12 or 3/13. Spending nights somewhere lately. Skipping school. Unhappy?**—and on the other side were call signs and names.

I shut everything down, then climbed out of the basement. I walked around the empty house until it was time to go to school.

NINE

At school, kids whispered around me. They stopped calling me "Vivian Ritalin" or hissing "sweatshirt" to tease me in class. They treated me differently, and so did the teachers. Everyone knew that Audra had disappeared.

I had stopped taking my pills by then, and I couldn't tell if I felt any different. I couldn't tell what my body might do as I sat there at my desk, looking out the window, surrounded by all these kids who weren't my friends. It was the middle of the afternoon in my English class. Mrs. Morgan had put a piece of cardboard in front of the clock, so it wasn't easy to tell what time it was, and I was hardly listening to her talk about *The Catcher in the Rye.* Instead, I looked out the window, over the sports fields, out to Grant Park, along Northeast 33rd. I could see the statues reflecting the sun there, the figures of Ramona and Henry and Ribsy. There was no Beezus, and no explanation for why there wasn't. I remembered the part when Beezus admitted she didn't love Ramona, even though everyone knew that's what sisters were supposed to do.

"Vivian Hanselman," Mrs. Morgan said. "Are you daydreaming?"

"No," I said. "Yes."

Everyone laughed.

The bell rang, and kids started closing their books, putting things away. Everyone went straight out the door, and I followed them, quickly enough that Mrs. Morgan wouldn't try to stop me, to ask me how I was feeling.

The first week or so after Audra was gone, Mom dropped me off and picked me up from school, careful like she didn't want to lose me, too. But then slowly that stopped and I could ride my bike again.

I unlocked it at the rack, rode out past the groups of kids. I felt someone's eyes, someone watching me, somewhere, keeping track; I saw Audra's face on bus shelters and telephone poles, the bright blue MISSING posters we'd hung up everywhere.

There was an old picture of Audra at a track meet, smiling, not looking at all the way she did when she disappeared, and another of her face where the copier made her eyes and mouth so black and you couldn't even see her nose.

MISSING
AUDRA HANSELMAN
17 Y.O. 5'5" 115 LBS.
HAIR BLACK EYES BROWN
NOSE PIERCING
CAMOUFLAGE CLOTHING
COULD BE WITH PERSON
OR PERSONS UNKNOWN

I rode, the books in my pack shifting on my back as I swerved around the corner, as I coasted down Siskiyou Street.

Audra's footprints still showed dark on the front of

our house, where she'd pushed off, when swinging. It was like she'd run up the side of our house and into the sky, or onto the rooftop, next to the window of her room. I stopped under the tree and looked up at her footprints. My handlebars knocked against the swing as I pushed my bike toward the garage.

Inside the house, upstairs, I swung off my pack and set it on my desk chair, unzipped it. I took out my biology textbook, then the yellow notebook. There, just below where I had written my questions, new words:

> *A wild bird can choose a person to follow,*
> *from place to place. A friend is a thing to*
> *learn how to be and always changing. A*
> *pencil sharpener, a paper clip, a stapler—*
> *now those are other weapons. The sea looks*
> *like metal, the sky like water. We saw*
> *you waiting for the bus with your sister,*
> *looking up and down the street with your*
> *hair in your face. That was a sweet sight,*
> *a pleasure to notice. Animals quickly take*
> *notice of white teeth and the whites of*

the eyes. During cold weather, the breath
should be directed along the body, so the
plumes of air are not visible to animals.
Blindfolding increases children's ability
to travel at night. Wisely take advantage
of new experiences. It's important to push
yourself beyond what you've done before.
Sometimes we're blindfolded without
knowing it, like horses we wear blinders.
There is a world beyond that of the five
senses, different than the realm of the
imagination. It is unseen, the world of
spirit and vision. It is a dimension of life
that very few people of today are aware
of, or perhaps care to know, one that even
fewer can access.

It was a relief to see those words, to know they hadn't stopped, and it made me feel good, too, because whoever sent them believed that I could be aware of the unseen world. I didn't know what that meant, but I wanted to believe that, too. It reminded me of the things Iceland had said; she had called me "special," which can be a compliment but sometimes it is a nice way of saying you're different, unable to do the things other people can do.

I felt different—I didn't need the messages to tell me that. I needed the way I was different to help me, to find my sister, to see things and understand things. I wanted instructions and information. What I was getting instead were riddles.

TEN

Without my pills, it was harder to fall asleep. I turned over one way, then the other. The house was quiet except for Mom sighing, in her bedroom, and the soft scrape of an antenna shifting on the rooftop, pointing across the sky to somewhere, someone else.

I opened my eyes, closed them, opened them again. Through a gap in the curtains I could see the tall trees across the backyard, the tops of them leaning back and forth in the moonlight. And there was another sound, then, a tight sound, a kind of rubbing. The swing in the front yard, it had to be, the rope where it was knotted around the branch, where it slipped a little and slid and squeaked when someone was on it.

Quietly, I pulled the covers aside and stood up. Barefoot, I crossed the hall, into Audra's empty room. I didn't turn on the light as I stepped close to the window. Below, outside, the black circle of the tire swing cut back and forth, back and forth, but there was no one on it.

I stood there watching. The moon was full, so the swing's shadow was another black circle, sliding along the grass, slower and slower, the swing finally coming to a rest, the shadow a still black puddle beneath it.

In bed again, I lay flat on my back, even though I can't sleep on my back; I didn't want one of my ears to be pushed into the pillow. I wanted them both listening. And what I heard, after a while, I wasn't sure if it was anything, but then I thought it sounded like a scratching, a soft slap, then silence, then another sound. What it sounded like was someone trying to climb our house, the wall of it, right under my window.

I stood up, next to my bed, not moving for a moment, listening. The sounds stopped, or I thought they stopped. My blood rushed around and around. I stepped closer to the window. My hand was shaking as I pushed one edge of the curtain aside, as I leaned in. There was no one looking in at me. My forehead against the cool window, I could see no one on the wall, no one close against the house. But then a shadow slid out across the yard, away from the house, so smooth and fast, startling me as it disappeared into the blackness under the trees.

I pulled the curtains closed again, just a sliver between them so I could see out, so someone out there could not see me. I watched, and at first there was nothing, or the way that everything was so still made it hard to see the pale face lit by the moonlight, surrounded by all the dark trees and shadows. Bluish white, turned up to the moon. I knew right away that it wasn't Audra—the body was too stocky, too thick. Then a hand came up, bare and white, waving and slowly motioning for me to come outside. It was a person, standing there, waiting for me.

I stepped away from the window, into the hallway; careful of the floor where it squeaks at the top of the stairs, I went down into the kitchen. My jacket was on its hook, my rain boots by the back door. I put them on, then slowly opened the door and stepped outside. It wasn't too cold, and the moonlight shone down, making the grass look soft silver as I went, my black shadow dragging alongside me.

When I reached the darkness beneath the trees, I turned in a circle, squinting, alone.

"Vivian." The voice was a whisper, a man's whisper, and I couldn't tell where it came from. "Vivian."

The second time, just as I figured it out, he slid silently down from a tree, ten feet away, and stepped close to me.

"Who are you?" I said.

"We need to get away from here," he said.

"If I scream, my dad will come. Their room is right there."

"Audra's waiting." He wore a black sweatshirt, black pants, so only his face and hands were easy to see.

"Where?" I said. "Why is she not here?"

"Come," he said, still whispering. "We have everything you need. Follow me, but not too close."

I followed him under the trees, almost tripping on

bushes and roots, and then between two houses, onto the street a block away from ours, Klickitat Street.

The sidewalks glowed, the moon bright and round above. We walked like that, with him half a block ahead, like we didn't know each other, until we were far from our neighborhood, on streets I didn't know. No one was out at all, in the middle of the night, no one driving their cars or anything. I had been waiting for this—I felt it, I realized it. I wasn't really thinking about what I was leaving behind, I was mostly just ready to start, to be with Audra again, to see what she'd found. And then the man turned and stopped walking and waited for me to catch up, so we could walk together, side by side.

"Okay," he said. "Are you all right?"

"Yes."

"This is good," he said. "Don't worry. I know about you, I have a feeling—"

"What do you know about me?"

"I'm just really happy you're with me," he said. "You're going to help us." He wasn't whispering anymore, and his voice was low, gravelly, lower than any voice I'd heard. Like it should belong to a man three times bigger.

"Where are we going?" I said. "Where's my sister?"

"Don't be afraid."

"I'm not."

As we walked, for a moment there was only the sound of my boots on the sidewalk. I saw that he was barefoot, and walked on the lawns of the houses that we passed, right along the edge of the cement. His dark hair was cut short, his skin pale in the moonlight, his nose thin and sharp. He probably weighed more than I did, even though he was shorter. It wasn't just that I was wearing boots and he was barefoot. His arms were longer than mine, though, swinging with his hands that looked too big on the end of his arms.

"In Audra's room," I said, "are those your hands that are traced on the wall?"

"Yes, they are," he said. "This way."

"Who are you?"

"I'm Henry," he said. "She never mentioned me?"

"Not your name."

"Well, the important thing is that we're together—the three of us."

"Where is she?"

"We're getting close, now," he said.

"Close to where?"

"When we get there, we can't talk, not at all. As we approach. Do you understand? This moon can make things more difficult."

I followed as we went down a side street that wasn't paved, that was only dirt with potholes, puddles shining like silver windows in the moonlight. Then he touched my elbow and tugged at my boots, the tops of them, so I knew to take them off. Carrying them, I crouched down low like he did, followed him off to the right, a narrow gap between two wooden fences.

As we got closer to a tall, dark house, we came to a place in the fence where the lower edges were not nailed in. He pulled them up, held them that way. My back scratched a little on the wood above, behind me, as I slipped through.

He followed, silent as he moved around me, as he kneeled down close to the side of the house. There was crisscrossing wood there that I learned is called lattice, that blocked off the space between the ground and the bottom of the house. He lifted a section of lattice away and set it down, and then waved for me to get down, pointed into the dark square opening beneath the house.

A face looked out at me, pale and smiling. It was Audra.

I was quickly down there, inside in that total darkness. I felt Audra's fingers brush my arm as I reached out. I got hold of her. I was trying to slow it, to breathe. I couldn't tell if I was becoming agitated or if I was only so excited. My head hit something hard as we slid over. Her hair in my face, sweet. My legs wrapped around her body and my ankles hooked each other like I could squeeze her in two. I felt her hands rubbing my arms, my face. I heard her breathing, a whisper, felt tears when she turned her head.

And then my hold slowly loosened, and I began to feel the blankets beneath me, the foam rubber padding.

"Okay," Audra said. "It's all right, now. Klickitat. Everything's fine."

I heard a click and then a pale light came on, a little lamp with masking tape wrapped around the bulb to make it dim. I saw then that Audra's hair was bleached, that it was blond.

"Try to breathe more quietly," she said. "You're gasping. Take it slow, Vivian."

In the shadows, as my eyes adjusted, I could see that the lamp was wired somehow into a square black box, the battery from a car, and I could see other car batteries stacked up against the brick foundation that was one wall of the space down there. The other three were lattice, but the inside of the lattice was covered in black plastic, so light didn't shine out.

Other cords stretched from the batteries, plugged into blankets, electric blankets, to a white-faced clock that hung from the wall. There were notebooks, there were Audra's books, library books. The ceiling was low—sitting there, I could reach up and touch it, close to the top of my head—and empty egg cartons and pink insulation were tacked to it, to muffle any sound we might make.

Beneath the twisted blankets were foam rubber mats, and a wool blanket hung down, separating the space. On the other side was my bed, my area, my clothes stacked there, waiting, even my orange life jacket, all the things that had been collected for me.

"I didn't panic," I said.

"I knew you wouldn't."

"I got the knife you left, but I left it, forgot it. I didn't know."

"We have plenty of knives," she said.

"I'm so happy," I said, hugging her.

"Enough," Henry said, behind us. "That's enough talk for now. We generally don't talk, here. And we don't use the lamp, really, unless it's an emergency." In that dim light he looked like he might be our age, or he might be ten years older, or even more. Somewhere between a boy and a man.

Audra reached out then, and touched his hand, just before he switched off the lamp, and the blackness was thick around me. In the darkness, I felt Audra shift past me, and then I heard a rattle, then a sound, the soft scratching of her writing, as she began to explain to me, writing down how things would be.

ELEVEN

That first morning I could already hear the two of them when I opened my eyes, the rustle of them on the other side of the wool blanket. I pushed it back and Audra was sitting there wearing only a black bra, a beige skirt. Henry sat next to her in a white uniform shirt with a patch from the QFC supermarket on his chest. He put on a blue apron, his black shoes in his hands.

"Audra," I said, and right away her hand was on my mouth, pressed against my teeth, and they were both looking at me like I'd done something wrong.

Then Audra took her hand off my mouth and picked up a spiral notebook—the one with the blue cover, one I still have, so now I can just copy down the conversation we wrote. She took a pencil from a jar, licked its black tip with her tongue.

Good morning, she wrote. *We're about to go to work.*

She handed the pencil to me, then pulled a blue blouse over her head while I wrote. She buttoned the blouse, pulled on a gray sweater.

I wrote: **Work? What am I supposed to do?**

Wait. We'll be back in the afternoon. Sleep all you can. There's a lot to read, to get ready for. I'm so happy we're together.

I can come with you. Where do you work?

Wait. Trust me.

But what am I supposed to do?

Trust us.

Henry had put on his shoes, now, tied the thin black laces. Audra pointed to a white plastic bucket with a lid snapped on, and then she wrote again.

That bucket is the toilet. There's food, everything. Just look around.

So I just wait?

Yes.

When she finished writing that, she didn't hand me the pencil. Instead, she put it in the jar, and reached for a pair of black shoes. Leaning close, she kissed me on the cheek. Behind her, Henry had moved the lattice aside, and she turned and crawled out after him. There was a glimpse of the bright morning, her hand waving, and then the lattice slid back across and I was left in the dimness, my eyes adjusting.

I opened the blue notebook. On the first two pages were the questions and answers between me and Audra that I'd already written down, and then more words, which she must have written after I fell asleep.

Vivian, we have been living in this place a short time and will live here a short time longer. We need to work to make money so we can leave, so we can move far, far away from here. We'll live in the wilderness. We'll be our own kind of family. You'll see we can trust Henry. He knows so many things that we don't know.

In the notebook's wire spiral were white snakes of paper where pages had been torn out. Pages where maybe Audra and Henry had written to each other, back and forth, but now they were gone, words I'll never know.

The pages after where I'd written with Audra were blank, but I shuffled all the way to the back. I turned the notebook over, and that's where I found a list, in Audra's handwriting:

~~Gym Membership (showers, training)~~
~~Bank w/ Alaska Branch~~
Seattle ➝ Ketchikan
Get V
Hand strength
Snare Training Ropes Duct Tape
Get New Name + SS# for V
~~Laundromat~~
Practice Knots
P.O. Box?
~~Picnic?~~
~~Socks/Underwear~~

I took out the pencil and crossed out *Get V* so it read ~~*Get V*~~. Then I closed the notebook and leaned it against the others in their box.

I don't know if it was a lonely day. There was so much to read and think about, and I was simply happy to be with Audra again, yet impatient to see what would happen next.

That first morning, I slid the curtain of the wool blanket to one side and looked around. The stack of car batteries, the cords stretching from them to the electric blankets, to the toaster. Three black plastic bags of clothes—I looked in them, and found that one bag was for me. Some of the clothes I recognized, Audra must have stolen them out of our house, somehow. Others were new, with tags still on them, my size.

I found a blue passport in a box. The picture of the girl looked a little like Audra, with her blond hair. The name of the girl was Janine Osgood.

Against the far wall was a kind of bookshelf, a board and two bricks to keep it off the floor, and on it the books missing from Audra's room. Near the toaster, a plastic bag of bagels that weren't too stale, and jugs of water to drink. There were some bananas, I think. We only ate food down there that didn't make any sound.

I lay back, closed my eyes, opened them. A little

morning light slipped around the edges of the black plastic, where it was attached to the inside of the lattice. I could see the beams of the floor of the house above, and all the egg cartons and insulation attached there to hide any noise we might make. I could sit up, crawl, roll back and forth. Back on my side of the space, I rested with my head on the orange life jacket.

I read, I slept, I dreamed and daydreamed.

What did I read, on that first day? I picked up *Journey to the Center of the Earth*, but I couldn't get into it right away. Instead, I read *Swiss Family Robinson*, slowly, from beginning to end. I liked the boat part, the wreck, and the special collars they made for the dogs, even though they killed so many things and even if all the brothers were hard to keep straight in my mind. I liked the animals, too, all the different kinds of animals they tamed and rode. They named the ostrich Hurry, which is a good name for an ostrich. It reminded me of the Boxcar Children's dog, who is named Watch.

That was what I was reading when I heard the footsteps. I stopped reading, like reading could make a noise, my thoughts might give me away. I held my breath, listening. Right overhead, they were coming nearer, then wandering away, standing still. Moving again. Could I hear a voice? A radio playing? I tried to imagine the person in the house above me, walking back and forth, but it was hard to know where to begin, with only the sounds. It could be a man or a woman, not a little child. Only one person, who might live alone. I listened for a long time, until I was certain there were no more sounds, that the person was gone.

As the day went on, thin stripes of sunlight shone in, narrow and bright along the edges of that space, and that's how I read, leaning close. If I pressed my eye against the edge of the lattice, I could see the green grass of the yard, bright yellow dandelions. A rusty shovel leaning against the wooden fence that was old and faded, some of the knotholes fallen out. Bright blue sky, just a triangle that I could see, clouds drifting past.

Inside, I followed a spider along the blankets, across the lattice and up, back and forth, watching all the time it took to make her web and also wondering what she hoped to catch, in this small, dark space.

I imagined Henry stacking boxes at the QFC, wearing his blue apron, his large pale hands going, and Audra out somewhere, hard to imagine because I didn't know what her job was, yet. Those two were out there working and they were the only people in the world who knew where I was. I wondered about my parents, about Mom and Dad, and it did not make me feel good to imagine them waking up and finding that I was gone. Were they walking and driving through the streets right now? Trying to talk with my teachers or the kids at the school? Making posters with my face on them and hanging them all around the neighborhood?

The lattice shifted, startling me, and slid aside. All the light shone in, in my eyes. It was Henry, coming back first. I slid back, out of the way, so that he could get through the opening.

He didn't say anything; he hardly glanced at me. He unlaced his black shoes and set them to one side, then took a comb from his bag and combed his hair, even though it looked the same when he was done. Reaching out, he picked up a book called *The Search*, and began to read. Later Audra would tell me that Henry could see in the dark, but that was the first time I saw him do anything like that and I wasn't sure he was really reading. I thought he might just be pretending.

Next, he set his reading aside and began to do a series of stretches and exercises. Audra would tell me that it was yoga, but that first day I just watched as he lay on his stomach, lifted his head and shoulders. He reached back to grab his ankles, his face pointing right at me and not looking. He twisted his arms behind his back, his neck all the way around so he could see behind him. He balanced on his hands, his knees on his elbows, his butt sticking up near where the egg cartons were attached.

I watched him. I didn't know if I was supposed to do something, to copy what he was doing, or not to watch him. And then he settled, again, and took out the blue notebook, and began to write. He handed it to me when it was finished.

His writing was all capitals, so small:

WHERE I COME FROM THERE WAS
A MAN WHO TALKED TO PEOPLE NO
ONE ELSE COULD SEE. HE PUT HIS
EAR TO THE GROUND AND TOLD US

SHIPS WERE COMING, OUT ON THE
SEA. SOMETIMES HE MADE SENSE
AND SOMETIMES HE MADE NO SENSE
BUT HE COULD READ THE ANIMALS
AND WAS THE BEST HUNTER AMONG
US. ONCE HE WENT ON A HUNT AND
DIDN'T RETURN. THAT'S WHEN OUR
LUCK BEGAN TO CHANGE, WHEN
EVERYTHING STARTED GOING
WRONG AND NOW THERE ARE SO
FEW OF US.

"What?" I said, after I read it.

Henry only put his finger to his mouth, which I took as a sign to be quiet but also that what he'd written was a secret.

And then there was a sound, the scrape of the lattice, and he tore the page from the notebook and folded it away, hidden in his pocket, just as Audra crawled in.

She hurried over to hug me. In that dim light her face looked smoother, no pimples or anything, than I'd ever seen it, and when she smiled it wasn't to tease me or joke about something. It was happiness.

She took the blue notebook to write to me:

> *I can hardly believe you're here. Did you have a good day? The whole time at work I was thinking of you. Now we're together. Once it's dark we can go out walking in the night.*

Next she took out a brush and brushed my hair, hard and straight, a sound that made Henry turn to look at us. She pulled back my hair in a ponytail and held it tight at the back of my head, her fingers circled there. It hurt a little, the pull on my scalp, and when she moved her arm, my head turned whichever way she wanted.

TWELVE

Later that first night we went out walking. Silently, carefully, we slipped out into the alleyway, into the dark streets.

The way we walked, we spread out, so we wouldn't be seen together, so we wouldn't draw attention. Henry led the way, fifty feet in front, wearing all black, his dark hair shining under the streetlights. His strides were long, his arms hanging down, his fingers out wide like he was ready to snatch something out of the dark air around him. He cracked his knuckles, and I heard it, so far away, following. I wore a black hoodie, the hood up, black sneakers and jeans, my hands in my pockets since the night was cold. Audra was half a block away, behind me, practicing all her different walks. On her toes, crouching down, arms out wide. Her blond hair hung down and made it hard to see her face.

It was only once we were farther from where we slept that we could walk alongside each other and talk. It was always Henry and Audra, or Audra and me, together; I never walked with Henry and I wondered if that was his choice, if he really had nothing to say to me. When we had been alone together, it felt like there was more he wanted to tell.

When he turned and waved back at us, Audra understood; she caught up to me, her face flashing for a moment under a streetlight, smiling.

"Now it's all starting," she said. "Now we can get going."

"Where?" I said.

"Far away," she said. "Far from any city. I'll take care of you."

"I thought you left me behind," I said.

"I'll always take care of you," she said. "No one else can calm you down."

We walked in silence, across a schoolyard. Ahead, Henry turned to check on us, then kept going, deeper into a neighborhood.

"Did you bring your pills?" Audra said.

"No," I said. "I haven't taken them for a long time. Actually, I haven't felt—"

"You'll feel better, now," she said. "And if it happens again, what happens to you, you can always hold on to me, do whatever you need to do. Henry, too. He knows. He understands. I told him all about you."

"What did you tell him?"

"At first he wasn't sure, I'm the only one he wanted. But when I told him about you, when he saw you, he changed his mind. He says we'll only really know what's going on once those chemicals are out of your system, once we get you away from all this—" She waved her hands at the parked cars, the houses around us.

I tried to touch Audra's hand, but when I reached out she didn't see.

"How did you meet him?" I said.

"He came looking for me," she said. "He needs me."

"For what?"

"For everything," she said. "To help him. To go with him, back where he's from."

"Alaska?"

"Who told you that?"

"I read it, in the blue notebook, when you were out."

"He's from way out in the wilderness," she said. "On the edge of the ocean. That's where we'll all be, and we'll live like we're supposed to, without all this plastic and cars and billboards and everything else."

With that she moved quickly away, catching up to Henry. The two of them moved like shadows, dark overlapping silhouettes. A dog barked, behind a fence. Lights in windows switched off, people going to bed.

We came to a thicket of trees, up above the river. Down below, near the old train tracks, was a bonfire, the orange flames and the dark shapes of people and bicycles around it, a dog sniffing back and forth. Henry waved to me, and I hurried to be closer to them.

"Remember," he was saying, "let me do the talking. This is one of the last things we need to do, and it doesn't have to get complicated."

We followed him, half walking and half sliding down

the slope, then came out of the trees at the bottom, together as we approached the fire.

"Keep to yourself," Audra said to me. "Tell me right away if anyone tries anything. Just stand by yourself while we do this."

Faces looked up, glowing and flickering. A dog rushed at us, sniffed my hand, slipped away. There were more than ten, less than twenty, people around the fire. Some had their shirts off, and some had tattoos on their faces, stretched-out earlobes. Some held pieces of bikes, cans of beer.

"Henry!" one shouted. "Where you been?"

Some of them started talking to each other, about Henry or about us, but I couldn't hear what they were saying. I stepped closer to the fire, not looking at anyone, staring into the flames. It was nice to feel warm, the front of my body all lit up and my muscles not so tight.

Henry's hands were up in the air, as he explained what he needed to explain, as he pointed back at me. He and Audra were close, just a little ways away. They were talking to two men where a cluster of people were standing. Little flames, lighters, flickered there, as the other people tried to light something, to smoke something.

A person stood next to me. At first I just looked at the feet, rubber sandals and dirty white socks, a hole in one toe. Torn-up jeans, a flannel shirt. It was a girl, shorter than me. Her black hair was all different lengths, jagged, and the mascara and makeup were thick black around her eyes.

"Who are you?" she said.

"I won't be here long," I said.

"That's your sister, over there?"

"Yes."

"I'm fourteen," the girl said. "My name's Taffy."

In the firelight, then, I could see the white line of a scar that stretched up out of her shirt and up around, back behind her ear.

"Henry," she said. "One time he talked to me. I still remember it. He reached out and held on to my arm, right here, and he said, 'It'll be all right. There'll be other people for you.'"

I just looked into the fire, the curling flames. I didn't say anything.

"Your sister's pretty," the girl said.

"She didn't always look like that," I said.

"You don't really look much like her."

"I said she doesn't always look that way."

"I had a sister whose name was Valerie," the girl said. "But she died."

"Was she older or younger?" I said.

"Johnny and Isabel were our parents," she said. "But they died, too."

Behind us, two guys started fighting. The dog barked and people shouted. Henry stepped over into the middle of the fight, then, and everything calmed down again.

"We're going away from here," I said.

"Where are you going?"

"I can't tell you," I said.

"And Henry, too?"

"Let's go!" Audra shouted, then.

"Good-bye," I said, stepping away from the fire.

I walked with Audra and Henry, out beyond the circle of firelight, past all the people, some calling Henry's name behind us. We started up the slope, back through the trees.

"Who was that girl?" Audra said. "I told you not to talk to anyone."

"Her name was Taffy," I said. "Her sister and her parents died."

"You didn't tell her your name?"

"No," I said.

"Her family got electrocuted," Henry said. "Up under that overpass, right over there. They tapped into an electrical line, and then there was a lightning storm, a surge."

It was too dark to see if he was pointing. The bushes and trees were thick.

"Her whole family?" Audra said. "Her parents?"

"Those weren't her real parents," Henry said. "It was a street family, one they made up."

"Is that what we are now?" I said.

"No," he said.

We started up the slope, the three of us finding our way through the trees.

"Do you have parents?" I said to Henry.

"Vivian," Audra said.

"I did," he said. "Not anymore. I have two brothers. They're younger—twins."

"In Alaska?" I said.

"We should get going," Audra said.

"Yes," Henry said. "That's where they are, but we don't call it Alaska. We just don't think of it quite like that."

"What do you call it?"

"Let's go," Audra said.

"Our families used to live in the city," he said, "in Alaska, and we left the city to live a different way, out by ourselves."

"You see?" Audra said to me. "Enough."

And then he climbed away, up ahead, gaining distance as we headed into the neighborhoods, out under the moonlight, the streetlights.

Later I'd find out that what we'd been doing at the bonfire was getting a new name for me, a Social Security number, an older age. The people Henry bought it from spent their days sorting through shredded papers, fitting those names and numbers together.

That night I didn't know that, yet. I hardly knew anything at all. All I could see was Audra and Henry ahead of me, their shoulders lightly bouncing together, and I was following them. Not too close, not too far away.

THIRTEEN

I saw Audra and Henry hold hands. I saw them lean close together. Beneath the house, the space was tight, so we were never far apart. There was the wool blanket hanging between us, but I could see their bare feet, down at the end, on top of each other, moving around. I knew what they were doing; I tried not to think about it, to imagine it. Sometimes I heard whispers I couldn't understand, but they never made much noise, even when they were moving around, and I couldn't see their bodies. I pulled my electric blanket up over my head.

Lying there, trying not to listen to them, I looked at my own body and I thought about what that girl Taffy had said. I was almost as tall as Audra, and almost as skinny, but my body didn't look like hers. I could tell it would never really look like hers. My chest would always be flatter, my shoulders wider, my hips not as wide as hers.

Audra and Henry left in the morning before it was light, and didn't return until it was dark out. I could read their work schedules in the blue notebook and I wondered sometimes what they did with all the extra time, early in the morning or in the late afternoon, whether they did things together or were alone.

I waited, and I was ready, but I was impatient, learning only a little at a time about what would happen. We were going to live out in the woods in Alaska, in the wilderness—if I didn't understand why we needed money to live like that, or why we needed passports, that was because I didn't know anything about precautions, about preparation.

While I was waiting, I tried to imagine what we were preparing for, what kind of family we would be. When I thought of the future, where we were going, all I could see was snow. I thought of Laura Ingalls Wilder in *The*

Long Winter, how Laura and Pa twisted straw into sticks because they had no firewood or coal to burn, no other way to keep warm.

I looked for clues to our future in the notebooks, but Audra and Henry wrote so few things down. Once, gathering dirty laundry, I did find a folded piece of paper, a note I kept and still have, something that Henry wrote:

> THE SCOUT OBSERVES A ROUTINE,
> FINDS THE WEAK POINT IN THAT
> ROUTINE, AND THEN ENTERS THE
> WEAK POINT AND MOVES WITH
> IT, THUS BECOMING INVISIBLE
> TO EVERYONE. THIS DEAD SPACE
> EXISTS IN BOTH NATURE AND THE
> CITY. EVEN THOSE PEOPLE WALKING
> ALONE AT NIGHT, FEARFUL OF
> ATTACK OR ROBBERY, FRIGHTENED
> AND HYPERVIGILANT, STILL HAD
> COUNTLESS DEAD SPACES IN WHICH
> I COULD OPERATE. EVEN THOSE WHO
> STALKED HAD THIS DEAD SPACE.

I'd read enough in Audra's Tom Brown, Jr., survivalist books to recognize that's where it came from. But Henry had copied it down, because it was important to him—he wanted to operate like Tom Brown, Jr., inside people's routines, tracking them, where they wouldn't expect and couldn't see him. Henry knew that there was so much beyond what we can see, and how important these secret spaces can be.

I looked for other words, as I searched through the notebooks, I hoped for messages like I'd received before. None came. My yellow notebook had been left behind, back in my bedroom; still, I had to believe that the words, the voices, could find me without that notebook, wherever I was, wherever we were going.

Maybe the voices would be there, where we were going. I thought of the note that Henry had written to me, about the man who talked to people no one else could see—it made me think that Henry understood, maybe, that he recognized how I was different. We would go to a place where I would never become agitated, where I could do so many things and the people would know that they needed me.

Lying there, waiting for Henry and Audra to return, reading *Journey to the Center of the Earth*, I could hear the woman who lived in the house above us. Her footsteps, in bare feet and then shoes, crossing rooms, back and forth. The clatter of pans, the sound of water in the sink, the water then rushing away, down through the pipes near my head. Henry and Audra kept track of her schedule, too, so we could guess when she would be home and when she would not, when we could come and go.

Journey to the Center of the Earth is a story that happens in Iceland. A boy and his uncle go down through the mouth of an old volcano that is named Snæfell. All the way under there they find lakes of black water, where they see animals caught back in prehistoric times. There are winds in the darkness. All the plants and flowers and trees are there, only they are gray and brown and faded because they never feel the warmth and light of the sun. The ferns are like black hands. The flowers, none of them smell like anything at all.

FOURTEEN

Henry and Audra, they came and went, and I was trapped underneath the house, waiting and wondering. When it rained it wasn't so bad, cuddling in my blanket and reading. In the corner of our space, down by my feet, water seeped in and puddled, muddy, but I kept my legs curled up, just listening to the rain against the wooden fence outside. When the sun shone was the worst, because I wanted to be out in it. Audra brought me vitamin D pills, and I didn't want to take them. How come some pills were okay, but not others? And how can you tell if you're feeling better, if you stop something that made you feel one way but every day you're waiting, hiding somewhere where no one knows where you are, when you want to be out in the sun?

Left alone, I would try to figure out what would happen, to imagine it. I went through Henry's things. He had almost no belongings, not many clothes. Just two pairs of pants that were exactly the same, and two white shirts, two pairs of socks. A black jacket. His work uniform.

One day in that first week, Henry came back early. He nodded to me, where I was reading; he spit-polished his black shoes, then set them aside. Next, he bent one leg up and twisted around to look behind him. He rested on his shoulders and pushed up with his feet, made his body bow upward, his stomach almost touching where the egg cartons were attached. He balanced on his hands, his knees on his elbows, his pale face turning red and his arms shaking.

I could hear him breathing as I read *The Foxfire Book*, looking at the pictures of the old women churning butter and weaving baskets, the toothless old men skinning rabbits, calling crows by blowing through special sticks. In one picture, a man and a black dog with a white chest were standing in front of an old shack. On the wooden wall of the shack a bear skin was nailed, and a fox skin, and four raccoon skins. I leaned in close, imagining that the raccoons were alive, only very flat, because the way they were hung there made it look like they were climbing.

I heard the scratch of a pen, Henry writing, but it took a moment to see that he was holding a folded piece of paper, a note, out to me. I felt him watching as I unfolded, as I read it.

EYES CAN TURN OUTWARD OR

INWARD

THERE IS A WORLD BEYOND THAT

OF THE FIVE SENSES

I folded the paper again and looked up at him.

"How do you know this?" I said.

"Be quieter."

"Did you write that?" I said. "Not that, I mean. The messages, in the notebook?"

"No."

"How?"

"I read the writing," he said. "In the notebook, in your room. . ."

We were whispering, a loud kind of whispering.

"When?" I said.

"You were asleep. We sneaked into your house, so I could see you, so I could decide."

"Decide what?"

"When I found the notebook, when I read those things, I could tell who you are, I could see that we needed you to come with us."

"Did you show Audra?"

"No. She was doing other things, I didn't tell her. Not yet. She can be jealous."

"What do you mean?"

"Listen. I need Audra, we need Audra. And you— it's like that man who talked to people no one could see, who I told you about. Not exactly, but something like that. You're a special person. You pick up on things that other people don't. We need a person like you. We will."

"Why?" I asked.

There was a sound—footsteps, above—and he paused.

"We can't," he said. "This is too much talking."

He pulled the wool blanket across, and I could hear by his breathing that he'd gone back to his yoga exercises. I tried to read *The Foxfire Book*, to focus, but my mind was imagining how it must have been that night in my bedroom: Henry reading all the messages with me asleep in my bed, so close, and Audra sitting at my desk and taking that cell phone apart, to show me that I hadn't been forgotten.

A little later, the lattice slid aside, and Audra crawled in, under the house. She looked at Henry, then at me—she could tell something was happening, had happened. She'd brought a loaf of bread, some carrots that we chewed quietly; things settled a little, in the air between us.

Henry lugged the plastic bucket out through the opening, into the alleyway, when it was time to go out walking. He dumped the bucket out in a porta potty at a construction site, a couple of blocks away, then left the empty bucket with the lid snapped on hidden where we could find it, where we could get it on our way back.

As he walked he was checking out all the cars and trucks he passed. What he was looking for, Audra told me, were older ones, ones where the hood could be opened from the outside, ones that had no latch inside the car or truck. Old cars and trucks, those were the ones he could steal the batteries from. He'd take them out quickly and stash them and we'd pick them up later, to use for electricity, beneath the house. She said you had to be careful, carrying them, since the acid inside could spill out and eat through your clothes, burn your skin. That made me think of my dad's old ski jacket, the one he kept in the basement, its stuffing showing through.

Out in the night the windows were lit, it was like a show, in the neighborhoods. I saw an old woman watching TV who scratched her head and then took her hair, her wig, right off. Families playing, kids wearing pajamas, running up stairs where I couldn't see them anymore. A fat man with black hair who seemed to be looking out but was only looking at his own reflection, his mouth moving like he was talking to himself or practicing saying something he wanted to say to someone. It was a little sad to see, I don't know why.

The light was on inside a car, and I could see a woman's head sliding through the night. Another woman fixing her lipstick in the rearview mirror, parked at a stoplight. A man with long hair in the car behind her, trying to read something on a strip of paper he held up in front of his face. If any of these people saw us, they would never know that we were together, the three of us, walking so spread out across the neighborhoods.

Audra drifted back and walked alongside me, Henry out ahead of us, a dark shape under the streetlights.

"Why don't I ever walk with him?" I said.

"You wouldn't have much to say to each other, anyway."

"Because he's your boyfriend?" I said. "Is that why?"

Audra laughed. "That's such a high school word! We're together, but I wouldn't call it that. He came to find me, because I was the one, and now we're together."

We crossed a shadowy park, stopping for a moment to sit on the swings. Henry waited for us, watching, standing on a deserted basketball court at the bottom of a grassy slope.

"What about me?" I said.

"You know I'll always take care of you."

Our shadows blended into the larger shadows of trees, then slipped out the other side.

"Maybe," I said, "maybe I don't always want to be taken care of."

"Vivian."

"Maybe I want to take care of myself," I said.

"You will," she said. "Of course you will."

The swings' chains jangled above, behind us, as we kept walking. The moon was almost full; it cast our shadows out into the street, our legs bending over the curb, our bodies and legs long and thin and black.

We climbed out of the neighborhood, into Mount Tabor Park, up past the reservoir, under the dark trees where the ground was steep. Our shoes in our hands, barefoot, we practiced how to step without making a sound.

Audra had her rope, her nylon cord, and her braided fishing line. She bent back saplings, little trees, tied nooses that attached to trigger sticks on the ground—I'd seen the drawings in the book, and she knew how to do it. Even in the low light I could tell she was smiling, that this was what she wanted to, what she liked to do. The snare would jerk an animal into the air, break its neck, but she didn't bait the traps, they were only practice. She took them apart, didn't leave them behind.

We spent hours in the trees, practicing for times in the future that I didn't know about. We raced to make shelters as quickly and quietly as possible; we played Blindfold Trap, where we had to set up a deadfall while blindfolded, where the trap always caught my hand.

The Rock Tool Game, the Throwing Stick Game, the Fast Fire Game.

Audra and I climbed high in the trees. We tied our hammocks to branches and swung there, close together. Below, Henry was working on his blind, a pile of brush he could hide inside. I'd read in the book where it said you had to let the blind sit for days, so the animals would get used to it, so they would forget that it had been any other way and return to their normal activities, but Henry was only practicing, keeping his skills sharp.

"Where did he learn how to do all this?" I said.

"Everyone can," Audra said, "where he's from."

"Does he tell you about it?"

"Yes," she said. "Some things. He told me he has a boat for fishing that's so camouflaged a helicopter flying over couldn't see where it's hidden. He told me there are places dug underground where the people go—places that no one could see, that no one could find unless they knew."

"Are the people hiding?"

"I don't know," she said. "I think it's the weather, mostly. They're only underground in the winter. There's houses in the trees, too, for when it's warm."

"And there's other people there?"

I peeked over, down below to where Henry was trying to move his whole blind; in the deep shadows, it looked like a bush was sliding along the ground by itself. Above, I heard the wings of birds, the wind in the trees. The branches were blacker against the darkness, but I couldn't really see anything. Nothing moved at all.

"He said he had brothers," I said. "So there must be people."

"There are," Audra said. "Only there used to be more and now there are very few."

"And that's why he needs us?"

"Well," she said, "he came for me. I forget, sometimes, that you've never been with someone, the way I am with Henry. It's hard to explain."

"How? Because you're in love or something?"

"You can call it that, if you want," she said. "But it's more, bigger—he needs me, I need him, so we can take care of ourselves and each other without all these people telling us what to do, how to be."

It was silent, then, for a moment. I remembered that Henry told me I was special, and I wondered if he had told that to Audra, too. I felt her hand along my arm; she gave me a gentle push so we rocked together, high in the trees. Closer together, farther apart, slowly settling.

"I was thinking of," she said, "I was remembering that time in Colorado, at Grandma and Grandpa's, when their little dog, Sonny, got his paw caught on barbed wire. One of his pads was just dangling. Grandpa took a wire cutter and snipped it right off, part of that dog's body. I picked it up and it was warm, rough on the side that had touched the ground."

"I remember," I said.

"He ran away, not long after that. Sonny did."

"What made you think of that?" I said.

"I don't know."

"I miss Mom and Dad."

"We don't have time for that. It doesn't matter anymore."

"But—"

Below, there was a low whistle, Henry's signal that it was time to go. We reached for the branches, we began unknotting our hammocks, then slid down, trying to land without making a sound.

The three of us moved silently out of the shadows, back down into the neighborhoods, the square windows of the houses shining against the night. Audra took Henry's hand, glanced back at me.

"You follow now, Vivian."

I did, along the dark streets, looking into the warm, shining windows of the houses we passed. In that moment, I wanted to be warm and dry, to walk through rooms. I wanted to open a refrigerator and have choices about what to eat. It had been so long since I had a glass of milk; I never thought I'd miss that. And there I was, cold, holding no one's hand.

Ahead, Henry and Audra were talking, but I couldn't even hear the sound of their voices. I felt very far away. I could tell that they were laughing, by the way their bodies moved.

I'd never seen Audra so happy; it made sense, her decision to be with him, to want to go away. She might not even have graduated from high school, if she'd stayed— even if she had graduated, the options weren't interesting to her. She wanted a new start, a different world. Me, I didn't know if the world I wanted was already hidden inside the one I knew.

FIFTEEN

The next morning, I lay listening to the woman walking around her kitchen, the scrape of a chair as she sat down, probably to eat lunch. It was Tuesday, around noon, and her schedule written in the blue note-book said she'd be going out soon. I waited. I listened carefully. When I heard her front door slam, when I heard her car start, out on the street, rattling as it drove away, I sat up and reached for my shoes.

In the alley, I ducked low, careful of the other houses. No one could see me, and soon I was out in the neighbor-hood, and anyone who saw me wouldn't recognize me. I usually wore my hood up, but by then we'd dyed my hair black, and Audra had cut it short, so I looked like a boy.

It felt strange to be out in the day, the brightness, to see all the colors and the edges of everything. I walked across town, back toward my school, my house, though that was not where I was going.

The lights were bright inside the QFC, all the colors of things to buy, the long aisles. I was looking in every direction, searching. Then, down an aisle, I saw Henry, stocking boxes of raisin bran. He wore his blue apron, a name tag that flashed in the light but that I couldn't read from far away. He was sitting sideways and didn't look over. His hands were fast, stacking those purple boxes, fitting them in tight.

I stood halfway into the aisle, watching him, not wanting him to see me, but he wasn't even looking in my direction. He wore a leather holster on his belt, some kind of gun in it that printed price tags or read bar codes. It swung a little as he turned away, walked down the aisle in the other direction. I followed, carefully, shoppers and shopping carts between me and him.

Henry went past the meat, all red in its cold cases, under the lights, past the pharmacy and pharmacists in their white coats. He went through a door with an

EMPLOYEES ONLY sign on it, leaving me to wait behind a round rack that held a hundred pairs of sunglasses. I could see my reflection in the lenses, so many of me with my short hair and everything. I hardly recognized myself.

When Henry came out of those doors—his blue apron off, pulling his white shirt untucked—he didn't see me. Of course he wasn't expecting me, and I followed as he began walking. What I wanted was to talk with him, and then also to see where he was going. I liked that he didn't know that I was following.

He walked out of the store, down toward the highway, and I followed, at a distance, as he climbed the stairs up over the MAX tracks, down onto the platform. Henry didn't look back, and there were people all around, waiting. When the train came, he got on, and I hurried to get on, too, one car behind him where he couldn't see me.

We headed into the city, toward the river. The train was crowded, people with suitcases coming back from the airport. At every stop I leaned close to the window, squinting out to see if Henry got off. He did not. We crossed the river, into downtown, past Pioneer Square. The stop after that, Henry did get off, and so did I.

With all the people on the street, it was easier to stay hidden but it was also harder to keep track of Henry.

There he was, buying a hot dog from a cart; that was a kind of food that we'd agreed not to eat, but he ate it as he walked, and I followed. Up the streets—10th, 11th, 12th—and turning right, going north—Flanders, Glisan, Hoyt. I practiced all the stalking techniques Audra had taught me, that I'd read about in the books, all the different walks.

After a little while I could see that he was headed to Forest Park, toward the thick trees. Forest Park is more like a forest than a park. A gravel road cuts through it for miles and miles, up the middle, but away from that road it's all thick and overgrown. Joggers and people on mountain bikes rushed close by. Henry didn't look back at me, still a hundred feet behind him.

If he turned, if he saw me, what could I say? I could only laugh, say I saw him and I was trying to catch up, that I needed some fresh air, that no one could stay under the house every day, all day, day after day. I would say that I was curious about him, that I wanted him to talk to me, to tell me about where he was from and where we were going, to talk about the messages in my notebook, to tell me why he needed me.

I almost called out to him; I waited, I followed.

Henry headed off on a side trail, into the shadows, and I had to hurry, to get closer. His white shirt flashed through the green leaves, his dark head rising and falling. The wind blew all through the branches up high and the trees groaned, rubbed against each other.

We climbed along a little ridge, across a steep slope. I kicked a stone by mistake and it clattered down through the ivy. I stopped, moved sideways, hid in the thicker bushes. Henry didn't turn. He was bent over, almost crawling now, heading off the path, up the slope. And then he stopped and bent down, and gradually—his legs, then his body, and then his head—he disappeared, down into the ground.

Slowly, carefully, I moved closer. When I reached the spot where he had been, I saw that there was a hole, there. Wide enough that a person could fit inside. I lay on my stomach, looking in. There was a candy wrapper in the shadowy bottom, but Henry was nowhere to be seen. I shielded my eyes with my hand, trying to understand.

Reaching into the hole, I felt all along the edge and realized that it was open along one side, a black tunnel slipping deeper underground. That was where he had gone.

I sat up and swung my legs around and slid over the edge, my feet hitting bottom, loose dirt falling and settling around me. Only my head stuck out of the ground, the rest in the hole, neck deep in the ground. Before I started down the tunnel, I turned slowly, checking in every direction, and that's when I saw him. Henry, again, heading off through the forest—he must have gone through the tunnel and come up from another hole. It wasn't easy for me to climb out, but I did, stumbling in the bushes after him, trying not to lose him.

I wasn't as quiet as I wanted to be, but still he didn't seem to hear me. He was looking up into the trees as he walked, and I was not far behind, carefully holding the bushes' branches out of my way.

I saw a ribbon, then, a blue ribbon, tied to one branch. I reached for it and at first I thought someone had grabbed my wrist—all at once my hand was jerked sideways, hard, up over my head. A thin cord ran from my wrist to the top of a tree, a sapling that had been bent back, sprung. As I tried to get loose, to twist free, I heard laughter behind me.

Audra came out from where she'd been hiding, coming closer to help get me free.

"It worked!" she said. "I caught you, Vivian. I tracked you and I snared you, too."

"You could have broken my arm," I said, rubbing at the red circle around my wrist. "My shoulder hurts, too."

"You'll be all right," she said. "And I'm learning these skills for your own good."

Audra wore a light green dress, like a polo shirt, only longer. Her blond hair was in two braids, and her skin was pale and smooth. It had been a long time since I'd really seen her in the daylight.

"What?" she said, turning around. "Why are you looking behind me?"

"Henry," I said. "I was following him, but I can't see him anymore. Are you meeting him here?"

"Henry?" she said. "I don't think so. He's supposed to be at work. Did he say something to you?"

"I saw him go into a hole in the ground," I said. "Into a tunnel."

"Vivian," she said. "You don't know what you're talking about. And if he's paying attention to you, that's because he wants *me* to be happy, to make you feel like he wants you along, too—"

"Okay," I said.

"What did he tell you?"

"Nothing," I said. "I followed him."

"You shouldn't follow him," she said. "You shouldn't even be out here."

"I had to," I said. "I can't stay under the house all day, every day—"

"Come on," she said, taking my arm like I'd done something wrong. "This way. I want to show you something."

We walked along a small, overgrown path, Audra leading the way. She held one hand up in front of her face, clearing spiderwebs, and I could hear that we were closer to the main gravel road, the sound of distant voices through the leaves of the trees and bushes.

"A lot of people live here," she said. "It's dangerous, it can be dangerous."

"Isn't this where the girl lived?" I said. "The girl we tried to find, with her father."

"Yes," Audra said. "Their camp wasn't so far from here."

"Did you ever find out where she went?"

"No," she said.

We walked silently for a while, farther from the road, staying close together.

"Things are different," I said. "The way we are together. It's not the same."

"Of course not, Vivian." Audra turned to face me. She put her hands on my shoulders, only for an instant. "It couldn't stay the same, now could it? And remember, the way things are now isn't how they'll be. We'll be able to talk anytime we want, and everything will be a lot better than now or before. You'll feel better."

I felt like we were in an argument that I didn't understand, that we hadn't had before. We walked side by side, then single file when the way grew narrow.

"But we're living underneath a house," I said. "I'm alone all the time, and you hurt my arm, and all we ever do is sneak around."

"That's not all we do," she said. "And it's just for a little while longer." She touched my shoulders again, turned me around to face the same direction as her. "You see that broken tree, and that green rock, there? It's exactly between them. Here."

We were standing right next to the blind she'd made—bent sticks with moss and leaves woven in—and it was almost impossible to see it.

"This is a safe place, in case anything happens."

"Like what?" I said.

"A safe place to come and stay," she said, almost whispering. "And there's a box buried inside, beneath it, with all the things in it we might need."

"In case we have to leave underneath the house or something?"

"Right," she said, "but it's not good to stay too close, too long, now, when we don't need it. Someone could see us, and wonder."

That afternoon Audra talked about awareness being the most important skill to have, and relaxation being the most important part of awareness. She waved her hands down over the distant city and talked about robots, about how unhappy people really were. She showed me some new things about tracking, and how to cup my hand around my ear, to make the shape of a deer's ear around my own, so I could direct my hearing better.

"Animals have acute senses," she said, "but if an animal has strong sight its ears are weak, or its sense of smell—humans have the best combination, if we just remember how to use them."

She blindfolded me, so I would listen harder. She took off the blindfold and showed me how to use my wide-angle vision, to switch from only looking straight ahead to also see the edges, the far corners of the world around me.

"Look out at the river," she said, pointing through a clearing in the trees. "Pretend it's a picture hanging on the wall, and push the frame out as far as you can, with your eyes."

"Is that a fishing boat down there," I said, "by the bridge?"

"No," she said. "That's a barge."

We stood there with our shoulders touching, looking out at the dark green river below, the pale blue sky above, the square reddish barge plowing through the water. I don't know which one of us started singing the song:

> Out of my window, looking through the night,
> I can see the barges' flickering lights
> Starboard shines green, and port is glowing red,
> I can see the barges far ahead
> Barges, I would love to go with you
> I would love to sail the ocean blue
> Barges, are there treasures in your hold?
> Do you fight with pirates, brave and bold?

That was a song Mom used to sing to us, when we were little, when she was putting us to bed. Singing the song made me miss her, and I knew that Audra was thinking of her, too. She didn't say so. She just leaned against me, and it was a little sad, but it was also a sweet time with my sister, standing close, singing with her.

"Hearing that song makes me think of Mom," I finally said.

"I know," Audra said.

"I miss her."

"Sometimes I do, too," Audra said. "That's all right. We don't have to forget her, it's just that we can't go back to how things were. We've made our choice, and we're meant to go somewhere else."

I didn't know what to say, so I only looked out at the river, feeling my sister's shoulder pressed against mine.

"The little girl who wrote that song," Audra said, "she was a girl in a wheelchair, who had some disease or some kind of accident, and she'd sit at her window and watch the barges and imagine all these adventures she couldn't have herself."

And then Audra sang again, a verse I'd never heard:

How my heart wants to sail away with you,
As you sail across the ocean blue
But I must stay beside my window clear,
As the barges sail away from here

Once it was dark we walked down out of the trees,

across the city, Audra half a block ahead and across the street so it wouldn't seem like we were together.

Henry wasn't under the house when we got there; he came back later, after I was already asleep.

SIXTEEN

The morning after I sang "Barges" with Audra, I woke up and listened to her and Henry heading off to work.

Later, I slipped out again, into the day. Rain misted down. Rain is helpful, since people squint through it, they look at the ground, they hurry. They don't stand or stare at something or someone they don't understand, try to figure it out. A person will look at you and in an instant decide who you are, line you up next to a person they know or a certain kind of person, so it is easy enough to blend in, to look a certain way where people's eyes slide right over you without snagging or hooking.

In crowds or on the train I would even stand next

to a lady so it looked as if she was my mother. Or I'd stand next to a group of kids that were horsing around so I looked like one of them. I watched and listened and smiled and I knew how to make my face light up a little like I knew them.

But I only mixed in crowds of kids if I was far from my parents' house, since I didn't want anyone to recognize me, and so mostly I walked by myself as I headed toward the QFC, toward Henry, because that was next to my old school, my old neighborhood. He would finish work in half an hour, and I planned to wait, then follow him again, to talk to him, this time.

On the way, I passed my old street. I stood there, at the end of our block. It was the middle of the day, a time my parents wouldn't be home, and so I decided to walk past. I had my hood up, and I didn't walk like myself. I scuffed my shoes along, like a boy.

The house looked the same from outside. The round window in the front door, the antennas sticking up from the roof, Audra's dark footprints high up on the wall, where she kicked when she was swinging.

There was no one on the street. Slowly, kind of walking backward to make sure no one was watching, I went down the driveway, around back. The cars were gone, all the windows were dark. I found the hidden key where it was always hidden, under the planter on the step of the back porch. You have to pull the back door toward you to get the key to turn, and I did that, then quietly pushed the door open.

And then, just like that, I was standing in our kitchen. It didn't smell right. The air felt sharper, cleaner, like chemicals. The kitchen looked the same, though, dirty breakfast dishes stacked in the sink. I walked through it, upstairs.

The smell was mostly coming out of Audra's room, where the door was open, and when I stepped inside, I realized that part of the smell was paint. All the walls were blue, now, the outlines of the hands painted over. The bed was pushed into the middle of the room, the mattress bare. The floor shone in the light from the window, like it had been scrubbed. The shelves were empty, the closet. I pulled open all the drawers and there was nothing in them.

My things were still in my room. My old books, some

of my clothes that I had almost forgotten, the orange blanket on my bed. First I opened the drawer, took out the knife Audra had left for me, put it in my pocket. Next I found the yellow notebook, in its hidden spot, tight in the bookshelf. I pulled it out, my hands trembling; I opened it up, paged through to find the new writing:

Suddenly we came upon a series of low subterranean tunnels that looked like beaver holes, or the work of foxes—through whose narrow and winding ways we had to literally crawl! Our bodies are so fluid, they can hardly be called bodies, they are made for where we are, and your body is changing. You are a special girl and will learn to camouflage your body, but also your mind and spirit so a person looking directly at you will not see you. Your sister can see you, is watching you, your body, mind, and spirit. The tunnels drift underground like clouds in the sky, they travel and cross each other. Will sisters travel,

cross each other? Hello again, calling
you! If you're caught in a situation with
wet shirt or denims, you can still warm
yourself by stuffing your shirt and pants
with leaves, grass, moss, fir branches. You
can also fashion emergency clothing items
from materials such as bark, rushes, and
cattail stalks.

I slapped the notebook shut, put it under my arm. I didn't want any of the other things in my room; I didn't miss them at all except for sleeping in my bed, just a little, and to be able to walk right across the hall to the bathroom, whenever I wanted to, having a toilet instead of a bucket with a tight snapped lid.

I crossed the hall, sat down on the toilet. The sound of me peeing was loud in the house. Above the sink in the holder were only two toothbrushes, blue and green, my parents'. Mine and Audra's had been put somewhere else, or thrown away.

After I finished, I sat there for a moment, and all at once heard a noise, a car outside. I stood to one side of the window, careful not to show myself. What would it mean, if Mom or Dad came home, found me there? Could I settle back in? Would I want to? I couldn't leave Audra, and Henry, who needed me; it wasn't as if we could have asked Mom and Dad, anyway, as if they'd let us go. We had made our choice.

The car passed, it wasn't our car—I could see the driveway and it was empty. I washed my hands, turned the water on and off again, then walked out past my parents' room. The door was open and inside it was all the same. The desk and a new computer, the same books on the bedside tables, my dad's asthma inhaler. If I was Audra I would have broken the computer screen, but I did not. Instead, I lay down on their bed for a moment, rolling my head onto one pillow, then the other, smelling how they smelled, so I would remember.

Downstairs again, in the kitchen, I took a pen from the cup next to the phone. I wrote a little letter, in my yellow notebook, then tore it loose:

I want you to know that we are together and we're doing fine.

We're happy. Don't worry about
us, and don't try to find us. You
couldn't find us because we've
moved far away to a place you
couldn't think of or guess. Thank
you for all your help in helping
us grow up.

    Yours sincerely,

    Vivian

Once I finished it, I realized that I couldn't just leave it there on the counter, since they'd know I had been there, and when. They'd know that I couldn't be too far away. So I found an envelope in the drawer and wrote the address of our house on it, and then I found a stamp. Only I couldn't put it in the mail slot because it wouldn't have a postmark on it and still they'd know how close I'd been. I slid the letter into my yellow notebook and then I went downstairs, into the basement.

When I turned on the radio switches, the lights came on in the tiny windows and the red needles bounced and settled. I put on the headset and had to close it down to make it smaller because it was adjusted for Dad's head. It made me miss him, sitting there in his chair with his old wool shirt on the back of the chair. The shirt smelled like him, its arms hanging down like they might lift up to hug me.

On a yellow pad of paper he'd written our names:

Audra   Vivian
                          *Woman reported
                          possible sighting on MAX
                          train, 5/12, but when
                          police questioned her
                          answers were uncertain
                          and she couldn't identify
                          V. with photos we
                          provided.

On the other side of the piece of paper, he had written:

Iceland says it is natural for girls
to wander. Of course she believes a
lot of things that are difficult to
believe.

In his logbook I found Iceland's call sign and I turned the dials even though as I did it I knew that would make the antennas on the rooftop turn and a person outside could see it and know that there was another person inside.

"CQ, TF8GX," I said. "CQ, Iceland. It's me, Vivian." I held the soft headset tight around my ears, but all I heard was static. I waited, but that did not change. I wondered how many people might be out there, listening to me, not answering. I wondered how many people were trying to talk to me, all at once.

And then I heard something else, cutting through that static. A ringing. I pulled the headset down and then I recognized it and I picked up my pack and ran up the stairs, back into the kitchen.

It was the telephone, and I reached out and almost answered it because I was used to answering it. I remembered, and pulled my hand back before I did. The answering machine played a message I couldn't hear, and then there was a beep. All I could hear was someone breathing, very softly, and then suddenly a voice, so loud in the kitchen.

"What are you doing in there?" a man said. "No, don't pick up the phone, Vivian. I know you're listening. I can see you standing in the kitchen."

I spun around, looking out the windows.

"You won't see me," the man said.

It was Henry, I realized. The voice was Henry's.

"As soon as I hang up," he said, "delete this message. Then go outside, lock the door, and return the key to its hiding place. Meet me at the corner of 33rd and Klickitat."

"Okay," I said, startled by my voice, knowing he couldn't hear it.

"Now delete this."

There was a click, and then I pushed the DELETE button so the light stopped blinking. I checked it and double-checked it, my fingers shaking.

I went out the back door, where the key was still in the lock. I locked the door, then put the key back in its hiding place. As I walked around past the garage, I slid my yellow notebook inside my shirt.

Henry stood where he said he'd be. He wasn't looking in my direction, but I could tell he was watching me coming.

"I'm sorry," I said. "I don't know why I wanted to go back—"

He leaned close to me, almost whispering, his voice so low and strange.

"Let's walk," he said, turning me by the elbow, so we faced the same direction.

"Is it okay," I said, "so close together, in the daylight?"

"Just this once," he said.

We headed away from my parents' house, away from Beverly Cleary School, farther away from where anyone would know me.

"You went back for the notebook?" he said. "I can see where you're holding it, there."

I didn't take it out from inside my shirt.

"Who do you think wrote those things?" he said.

"I don't know," I said. "The words just showed up. Like, it was closed, and when I opened it, they were there."

"That's what I thought." His hand brushed against mine, both swinging between us.

"How did you know?"

"Keep walking," he said. "Look straight ahead."

We passed a blue mailbox. I felt the notebook's spiral against my skin and thought of the letter inside it, the one I'd written to my parents.

"What would someone think," Henry said, "who saw us walking like this?"

"We probably look like brother and sister," I said.

"Or brother and brother," he said, "with that haircut of yours."

"Don't tease me," I said.

"I'm not," he said. "I like you." His hand brushed against mine, and he smiled.

I realized then that I hadn't turned off the radio switches, that all the windows would be lit already the next time Dad went into the basement, the dials turned to Iceland.

"I followed you, yesterday," I said. "Up to Forest Park."

"I know," he said. "I knew."

"I saw you go into that tunnel."

"So?"

"So what's that about?"

"The tunnels?" he said. "I found them. I don't know who made them, or what they're for, but they remind me of home, a little."

"Where you live in tunnels?"

"Sometimes, in the winter. You'll see."

"So," I said, after a moment. "You knew I was following?"

"Yes," he said. "And I saw you with Audra, and I listened to the two of you singing."

"Why did you hide from us?"

"You two need some time together," Henry said. "To sort things out, how things will be. Audra's not comfortable yet, with the three of us together. She can get a little jealous."

"Of me?" I said.

"It's not always easy for her. She's getting used to it—"

We walked. His hand brushed against mine again, and this time he held it.

"I want to take you out in my boat, fishing," he said. "The ocean rises and falls, just like it's breathing. The water's so cold, there. I'll teach you about it. I'll teach you to dry the salmon; we'll build the racks, out along the beach."

After a little while, half a block, it felt nice and not surprising, Henry holding my hand like that.

"These words that come to you," he said. "I think they'll make more sense when we get there—that's how we'll need you. To say when the ships are coming, and where the animals are hiding, to tell the people about all the things we can't see, and what will happen. We've been without a person like you—that's one of our problems."

We walked silently along, our arms swinging. The sun was bright and warm, not too hot. Our fingers were together and there was the smallest space between our palms, like we were holding a tiny, secret thing. I had never really been able to hold hands with someone for so long without becoming uncomfortable.

"But what if it doesn't work that way?" I said. "What if the words still don't make sense, and I can't do those things?"

"It doesn't help to worry about that," Henry said. "I need you to come. And anyway, Audra won't go without you." He looked up then, squinted at the sun. "She's waiting," he said, leading me through the neighborhoods, letting go of my hand. "We should get back."

Silently, we hurried toward the house.

Audra didn't like it, seeing Henry and me come back together, crawling under where she was waiting. She didn't really look at us, just kept shuffling things around.

I wrote to her in the notebook, **KLICKITAT**, but she wouldn't look at it. Henry just started stretching, balancing, doing his yoga exercises, and then Audra pulled the wool blanket across so I couldn't see them anymore.

I didn't know what to do. I didn't know if she saw Henry and me holding hands, or what. I just sat there, afraid of agitation coming over me, afraid that if I tried to hold on to her she wouldn't let me. For the first time since we'd been together again, I put the orange life jacket on and cinched its straps tight, to hold me. But the agitation didn't come. Instead I lay there worried that Audra was mad at me.

I heard the scratching, the scribbling, as they wrote back and forth in the notebook, having a conversation, an argument.

SEVENTEEN

When I woke up the next morning, I was alone.

I opened the blue notebook, but almost all the pages were torn out. At the very end of it, beneath where I'd written **KLICKITAT**, I saw that Audra had finally answered me, while I was asleep: *KLICKITAT*. Then I knew that we would be all right.

I fell asleep again, and when I woke up it was daytime, afternoon, and I was still alone. I stretched out, kicking off my blankets. Above I could hear the woman's footsteps, then silence as she stopped moving, then the water running. I got used to the sounds she made, so I could guess and imagine what she was doing. Making her coffee, toasting her toast, washing her dishes, all without knowing what was beneath her feet. I even figured out the sound of the cat jumping from the kitchen counter to the floor. His front feet, then his back ones.

After everything had gone silent for a while and I knew she was gone, I put my yellow notebook, my knife, and a sweater into a pack. I crawled out into the bright sunshine.

Henry didn't come out of the QFC when he was supposed to, and I got tired of waiting and went inside, walked up and down the aisles of mousetraps and ant poison and Ajax cleanser, past rows of bread and English muffins that made me hungry. The aisles of cold things where the air was cooler, all the frozen things to eat behind their glass doors.

A tall, bearded man in a blue apron began to follow me. He straightened things on shelves, keeping me in sight as I circled the aisles, walked through the produce. I turned around when he wasn't expecting it.

"I'm not a shoplifter," I said.

"Can I help you find something?" he said.

"No," I said. "Actually, I was looking for Henry."

"Henry?" The man made a face that was a kind of a

frown and walked away, and for a little while I thought he'd gone to find Henry, to bring him to me, but he didn't come back at all, so I headed outside again.

Audra—all I knew was that she worked at a Fred Meyer. I didn't know which one, except that she had to take a bus to get there.

When I saw a blue mailbox, I took out my letter and mailed it—after all, we'd be far away soon, probably by the time Mom and Dad received it—and I kept walking, all the way to Mount Tabor.

I found the practice blind that Henry had made, and climbed the tree where Audra and I had swung in our hammocks. I sat there, where no one could see me. I took off my backpack and hung it on a branch. Far away I could hear a ball bouncing, voices, and then the sounds drifted away.

Through the branches I could see the city, the long straight line of Hawthorne with cars—red, blue, yellow, all pale in the late day sun—driving on it, toward me and away from me, all the way across the bridge, downtown.

Closer, then, I saw a ragged bird watching me, loose feathers on his wings. Sitting ten feet away, on a branch, hopping a little closer. It flew away when I moved my hands, and it circled around and landed close to me. A little brown bird, some kind of sparrow, its neck jerking around so it could see in every direction, so it wouldn't be surprised. It lifted one little foot, then the other, perched there.

"What?" I said, and then I climbed down and began walking out from under the tall trees, past the playground, people on bikes and jogging along with bottles of water in their hands. Mount Tabor used to be a volcano, long ago before Portland was a city, and I sat on the grassy slope up above the square reservoir, waiting for the safe time to go back to Audra and Henry. Down below, two guys who were teenagers or older were practicing on the soapbox derby track, and a girl was with them. Their car was made out of a mattress and bicycle wheels, and had trouble turning the corners. It kept crashing into the trees.

People pushed strollers around the reservoir. The sun was going down and the cars were turning on their headlights. Far away down Hawthorne I could see the lights on the Bagdad Theatre and for some reason all at once I began to cry because I knew I was about to leave the place where I'd grown up and the parents I'd known and everything else. It felt so strange to be crying, to feel the tears on my face. I couldn't stop and I felt stupid.

At last I wiped my eyes and looked around until I saw the moon, so pale, and then I stood up and began walking back toward the house. Enough time had passed where it was safe again.

It was dusk, and harder to see, tears still in my eyes. Henry and Audra had taught me that it was never truly safe, and so as I got closer to the house I went slowly. I came into the alley the opposite way from how I usually did, and I stayed so low, my fingers brushing the ground in front of me. I could see there were no lights on in the house, and I slowly pushed out the loose part of the fence, backing up as I saw what had happened and then waiting to see if there were any voices, anything, after I moved the fence and stuck my head through.

Nothing happened, and I peeked through again. The pieces of lattice were gone, and a wide yellow plastic tape was wrapped around where it had been, around the space where we'd been living.

POLICE LINE: DO NOT CROSS

And our things—the foam rubber mats, the car bat-teries attached to wires, our blankets and clothes and books, my orange life jacket, our toaster—were scat-tered around the yard. They looked sad and sorry, spread out like that.

Quickly, I crawled through the gap and grabbed the blue notebook, as many of Audra's books as I could carry. Back through the fence, I zipped it all up in my pack and kept moving, away, back out into the night.

When cars passed, I hid behind trees. When lights came on in the windows of houses, I ran.

I took the MAX downtown, across the black river, and when I got out I kept walking, checking behind me and all around as I reached the even darker darkness under the trees, to Forest Park. It was so hard to see, to find my way, even though the moon was out. I pretended that it was the day I followed Henry, that he was just in front of me, and that helped me find my way. And then I wondered if he might be behind me, with Audra, watch-ing and following like some kind of test.

Vines tripped me. Branches scratched my face and hands. As I went, I kept expecting a snare, to have my arm jerked away, to fall into a pit, to have my legs swept out and to be hanging upside down, high in the trees, swinging in the darkness.

It took a long time, circling and circling, but my eyes adjusted a little and at last I saw the broken tree that Audra had shown me, before, and the green rock that was now black with shadows. I dropped down and crawled until I found the blind. I went inside. No one was there. I took off my pack and lay down, resting my head on it, waiting.

No one came. There was only the silence of the forest, which is never quite silent. The cracks of the trees, the scratching of branches, the wind, little animals scurrying about, and sounds that might be footsteps, that end and don't start up again.

This was where Audra and Henry would come for me, but that didn't mean no one else knew about it. Carefully, quietly, I brushed at the ground with one hand, clearing dirt and leaves from a board, which I lifted aside. Beneath it was the plastic box Audra had told me would be there. I took it out, pulled off the tight lid, felt around with my hand until I found a headlamp, its strap around my wrist. When I switched it on, I cupped the light in my hand, so it wouldn't go far. I could see some rope, and matches, some camping food. The hammock was wound tight, smaller than a shoe. I took that out and I took the foil emergency blanket out. I set them aside.

Then I unzipped my pack and pulled out some of Audra's heavy books. There was room for them in the box, and I put them in and snapped on the top and covered it over, brushing the dirt and leaves across again.

I didn't want to stay too close to the blind, and I didn't want to go too far away from it, but I knew if I fell asleep anyone might sneak up close to me. So I went a ways away, close enough that I would still be able to see the blind when I woke up, in the daylight. And then I began to climb.

The knots I knew, I'd practiced them so often in the darkness under the house. Tying them, I told myself that they would hold me, that they could hold a lot more weight than me.

I swung there, fifty feet from the ground in the hammock's braided strings, wrapped in the thin emergency blanket that held all my heat in. I was so frightened, up there alone without Audra swinging next to me, explaining how things worked, how they would be. My shoes hung from their laces, closer to the tree's trunk, and my pack was hooked there, too, still within arm's reach. I heard dogs somewhere, barking, then crashing through the brush, below, the sound of them slowly fading away. An owl, not too close. The creaking and settling of the forest.

EIGHTEEN

The sound of birds, that's what woke me, and the pink glow through my eyelids, the coming daylight. I opened my eyes slowly, and turned my head, squinting down between the strings of the hammock, the thick green of the leaves. I wouldn't have seen the blind if I didn't know it was there. If someone was inside it I wouldn't be able to see them from where I was.

Would they be able to see me? No, unless the sun came over the ridge and lit on my silver blanket, lit me up to reflect like a mirror. I pulled the blanket loose, crinkled it up in my hands as quietly as I could, shoved it into my pack.

It took me a while to get down, my hands shaking on the tree branches, the ground so far below. Once I'd done it, I stayed barefoot. I circled around the blind, came in from the other side, but there was no one there to surprise, no one there to sneak up on.

I dug out the box, sorted through the things it held. The headlamp, the food. Maps of Forest Park, and of the United States. Iodine tablets for water. A green bandana. A compass and a knife that I'd seen Audra use before. Toothpaste, a green toothbrush still in its package. A pair of jeans and a fleece shirt with a plastic thermometer on its zipper. Those were both my size. Socks and under-wear, also for me, no clothes for anyone else. They must have already been here, I decided, Audra and Henry have already taken their things.

I'm here, I wrote on a scrap of paper. **Back soon. V.**

I left that note in the box, buried the box again, then put on my shoes and began to circle, spiraling out from the blind, moving slowly. I found animal holes, even one small enough for a snake, but the tunnel I'd seen Henry go into was not so easy to find. I pulled branches aside. I waited for the sounds I made to settle.

It was in one of those moments, those pauses, that I heard the voices. Not too close, and no words that I could understand, but a sound that was more than two people, more than three. I took off my shoes and crept closer, using the Fox Walk that I'd learned from Audra, that she'd learned from the books.

When I got close, I could see into a clearing where four men sat next to a fire, passing a loaf of sliced white bread, each holding a piece in each hand. A rope was tied around a dog's neck, who sniffed at the ground, close to two skinny men and a woman who were sorting out scraps of shredded paper. There were tents made from blue tarps, and a bicycle resting on its handlebars and seat, its wheels in the air. Two shopping carts, piled high, covered with blue tarps. And near them I saw her, a girl I recognized, her ragged black hair and black makeup around her eyes that made them look huge, from where I was, like holes instead of eyes.

I eased backward, went all around the edge of the

clearing, keeping my distance and then coming up close behind her. What she was sitting on was like a bench, a seat taken out of a truck and dragged into the forest. She was eating an apple and not really looking at anything. It's hard to hear when you're eating, and I got close, ten feet away, watching her, trying to see if she seemed worried or scared, if this was an unsafe place for a girl to be.

I slipped out of the bushes and sat down next to her. She looked at me like she really wasn't that surprised.

"There you are," she said. "People are all looking for you."

"Who?" I said.

"Officer," she said. "Asking all the kids if you're around."

"You didn't say anything?"

"Of course not," she said. "And I haven't seen you for a while, anyway. You want a bite of apple?"

I did.

"It's a little sour," she said, watching me chew. "How'd you find me?"

"By accident," I said.

"You're barefoot."

I put my shoes on. The men at the fire looked over, but they didn't come closer or say anything. The other people, sorting the paper scraps, looked familiar. I think they were the ones who sold Henry my new Social Security number, my new name and age.

"Your name's Taffy," I said. "Right?"

She wore the same rubber sandals, now with no socks. Leaning forward, she scratched at a scab on her ankle.

"I know your name," she said. "It's Vivian."

"I don't care if you know my name. That doesn't matter."

"These people aren't anyone." She pointed into the clearing. "I'm not with them. I'm looking for someone to go with, but I'm doing all right by myself, right now."

"In the forest?"

"I wouldn't stay here at night," she said. "I have to be careful, in case someone's looking for me."

"Who's looking for you?" I said.

"I just have to be careful." She looked away, into the trees. "Last night, I slept in a parked car, in the back, and when I woke up it was driving. The lady never noticed me, but I had to walk all the way here from Lake Oswego."

When she leaned back, our shoulders were close together. She smelled like a fire, smoke, and some sweet deodorant. Her fingernails had red polish on them that was mostly scratched away.

"What about you?" she said.

"What?"

"Where's your sister? Where's Henry?"

"They're meeting me around here," I said. "Soon."

A gust of wind shook the branches, all around the clearing. The spotted dog barked, looking in every direction, then settled down again, tried to eat a hamburger wrapper. Taffy took back the apple and ate it all, the whole core, the stem, and the seeds.

"Have you seen her?" I said. "Have you seen Henry?"

"Not lately," she said. "I heard a lot about him, and then I saw him around. He talked to me, that one time." She leaned forward, back again, her shoulder against mine, then inches away. "I remember when I first saw your sister with him, so tall and beautiful with that hair and those clothes. They hardly looked like they could know each other."

"Well, they do," I said.

"A lot of people didn't like your sister," she said. "Just because of Henry and all his attention going to her and none to anyone else. People said she'd take him away."

She turned, so close, and stared at me like she was remembering my face. Her eyes, circled by that eyeliner and mascara, were pale blue, bloodshot. A pimple on the side of her nose. Her teeth were crooked, yellowish. She smiled all at once when she could tell I was looking at her.

"Sisters," she said, after a minute. "My sister Valerie, I only knew her about a year, and now I can hardly remember what her face looked like, you know?"

"I remember Audra's face," I said. "And she was my real sister. We had the same mom and dad, and we grew up in the same house. We were a *real* family. So I would never forget her face."

"Okay," she said. "I was only saying."

"I need to go." I stood up, swung my pack up over my shoulders. "I know what to do in the woods because I've been practicing. I've read a lot of books. There's a lot of things about how things work that we've just forgotten, living the way we do."

"I'll come along with you, then," she said.

"No," I said.

"Then why'd you come and sit next to me?" she said.

"I wanted to see if you were all right," I said.

"Really?"

"Good-bye," I said, and slipped back into the bushes, back the way I'd come.

After a short time I doubled back, in case she'd tried to follow, but she was still sitting there in just the same way. Still, I was careful. Barefoot again, I walked only on stones and roots, leaving no footprints as I went deeper into the forest.

I practiced Fox-Walking under the trees, trying to be aware of everything, all the sounds and movements around me.

I leapt a stream. I climbed a tree, moved from its branches to another's. It was then I saw something in the branches of a farther tree. A platform of old boards and branches, a kind of tree house high in the air. It even had old vines and brush attached to its bottom, to make it harder to see. At first I thought the tree house might be Audra's, but when I climbed closer I saw it was different than one she would make, more broken-down.

I climbed up there, onto the platform. I took off my pack, and rested. It felt so much closer to the sky, and through the trees I could see the river, the bridge, the boats. I didn't sing the barges song. Instead, I opened my pack and took out my water bottle.

I noticed the words, then. Words were carved into the boards I was sitting on.

friend
friend
friend

For some reason, reading that, I knew all at once that this tree house had belonged to the lost girl, the girl who lived in this forest with her father. I knew that she had carved those words, that word. Caroline. Caroline. Caroline.

I unzipped my pack's front pocket and took out the

knife Audra had given me. It was sharp, because I sharpened its blade every morning. In the tree house I lay flat on my stomach and held that knife like a pen as I slowly carved my word.

KLICKITAT

NINETEEN

I kept thinking over what had happened, why Audra and Henry had gone, and where, all the possibilities. It was possible that they had been found out, caught, and taken somewhere. With all the planning and precautions, that seemed almost impossible, but it was still a possibility. If they were caught somewhere, they would get out, and then they would come for me. They could not leave me. But I knew that, at the same time, they had no clothes hidden in the blind for themselves, they had left nothing of their own behind. That was hard to understand.

I imagined what I would say to Audra if she were next to me, swinging in the hammock. I don't think I would have told her about sneaking into our house, about her bedroom painted blue. I would have just reminded her how we are sisters, how she could help me calm down and settle, how when she got hurt she didn't want anyone else around her. I thought about the sunny corral at my grandparents' ranch in Colorado, the round metal water trough with a dent in one side. Two thick orange fish always swam in it. The trough was dented because Audra once climbed onto Duke, the old blind horse, and he'd bucked and kicked the trough as he threw her off. She didn't break her leg, but she hurt it. She didn't have stitches in her forehead, where they thought she might. She had a concussion, though, and headaches, and I was the only person she wanted around. She wanted to sleep with me in one of the twin beds in my dad's old room from when he was a boy. We stayed in there and my grandma brought us burnt toast and chicken noodle soup. This little dog they had—he ran away, later, but when Audra was hurt he'd sit on the other twin bed, watching us, wagging his tail if we said his name.

It also seemed possible to me, swinging in the hammock in the tree's branches, that Audra was still angry, that she and Henry had a disagreement about me. Was she jealous of me? Did she not want to share Henry, or to share me? Had he told her about the messages, my notebook, and she was jealous of that?

If she was angry with me, that anger would pass. When she'd left me before, she'd returned; she couldn't really leave me behind. Still, I worried. If I was left behind, alone, what did I have? Maps, my yellow notebook, iodine, books of survival skills.

Nothing was as easy as the books made it seem. I couldn't find the plants I read about, or the berries to eat. I dug up roots and washed them in the stream and then I wasn't sure if I should boil them, or what I should do. Mostly I was eating the dried ramen noodles and jerky, the bars and nuts, left in the plastic box. I didn't know how long it would all last.

It was harder not to think of Mom and Dad and my bed, of all the food in the refrigerator, when I was alone. I knew that a good attitude was important in a survival situation. I knew not to panic. I knew it was best to keep myself busy, to believe that Audra and Henry would return very soon. I set out on long walks. I practiced my stalking and my other skills, climbed from tree to tree, tried to find plant fibers to braid into cords and ropes.

The first tunnel I found, I heard it before I saw it. A low kind of whistle coming out of the ground. I crawled closer, to a spot beneath a bush, deep in a thicket, and felt the cool wind on the skin of my face. It was gentle. It smelled like dirt and stone.

This was on the second day.

The mouth of the tunnel was just a jagged black opening, big enough to fit my hands inside, to pull rocks away, to push them until I heard them rattle below. It took a little while—I set my pack to one side to dig, and I didn't have any tools to dig with—but at last it was wide enough to stick my head inside, to shine the head-lamp down. I stretched one hand deeper, too, and felt that it wasn't only a hole, or an animal's den. It opened, on one side, and that's where the wind was coming from. A tunnel.

I lowered myself inside, feet first. Only my head was above the ground, and I pulled my pack in after me, ducked my head, and started into the tunnel, deeper.

It slanted down, and soon I could stand up, the ceiling still close, cold water dripping on my head, puddles beneath my feet. The walls were close, too. I couldn't stretch my arms all the way out.

How far did I go? I thought of the story we read in school, about the man in the labyrinth and the ball of string that kept him from getting lost. I had no string, but in this cave, this tunnel, there was only one passage, no others forking away in the darkness. I checked. I kept turning my head from side to side, the headlamp's beam sliding across roots and stone, crumbling black walls of dirt.

The floor sloped up or the ceiling sloped down. I hit my head. Bending lower, I had to crawl again, had to switch my pack around to the front, on my chest, since it kept snagging on the ceiling. The stones were sharp against my hands and knees. I didn't care. And the wind, I was still heading into it, started to blow a little harder, to smell different. Not so thick with dirt and rocks, but cleaner, like trees and sky.

I switched off the headlamp and squinted ahead. After a little while I saw light, a jagged greenish opening, and I kept crawling toward it.

I had to dig my way out, a little, and when I stuck my head into the light it was too bright at first and I couldn't see at all. I coughed, breathed in as much air as I could, just sitting there in the tunnel's other mouth.

Slowly, I checked around myself. A bird, just at the side of where I could see, fluttered away through the green trees. I recognized where I was, which part of Forest Park. Far from where I'd gone into the tunnel, near where I'd been searching, earlier in the day, where I'd sprung one of Audra's old snares—a snap, a whistling sound, a loop of rope suddenly jerking empty through the air.

I quietly made my way toward the blind. I kept my eyes to the ground, checked the branches of the trees. Blackberry vines scratched the skin of my arms, my hands, and all at once there were voices, close by. I crouched in a bush, slowed my breathing. I waited until the air was silent again.

Sitting in the blind, I ate a dry square of ramen, drank from my water bottle. And then I began to cry. First only tears, and then more, all curled up on my side in the leaves and dirt. Even if I knew they'd be back, that Audra and Henry would come for me, I was lonely, and being left behind this time was worse—the first time, Audra was also getting away from our parents. This time, she was only getting away from me. I tried not to make noise, to stop crying or to teach myself to cry silently.

I found the yellow notebook, opened it; I paged in from the back, through the blank pages, into new words:

> It will be a bad winter if the crows gather
> and squirrels build their nests low in the
> trees. Hello hello hello. Nothing stands
> still, weather guides us. If worms are
> bending up and going into people's houses
> and abandoned buildings in October, the
> winter will be hard. Don't forget me, sister,
> believe I'm with you always. The number of
> days old the moon is at the first snow tells
> how many snows there will be that winter.
> A blanket of deep snow can keep you
> warm. Depths can be sounded by bouncing
> signals along the ocean floor.

These words didn't help, they only frustrated me.
I put the notebook away and rubbed my eyes to get the
tears out, so I could see. I couldn't let myself get sad like
that. I had to believe that Henry would come back and
take me to his people, so I could understand the words in
the notebook better, and then I'd be helpful to everyone.
But now the sky was turning dark.

While I climbed to the hammock, I realized that I had
hardly said a word all day. If the days went on like that,
would I lose my voice, be unable to talk to Audra? How
many days would it be before they came? I thought of how
I used to sing, how I liked to sing. At school, singing all
together where I could hear my voice small and close to
me and then blending into the noise that was everyone's
voice, pushing back on me in a comforting way.

The hammock, it held me tight, it calmed me. There
was a way to double the rope that was knotted to the
tree, to double it back and lace it through the braided
strings, to pull it tighter around me, to hold me.

Here I was, high in the trees, swinging gently against
the black sky.

Radio waves travel farther at night, without so much

interference—Dad told me that, one time down in the basement. I was folding laundry and he was sitting at his radio, turning dials and knobs. I didn't want to think about him, didn't want to start crying again.

I rested there, not quite asleep, listening to the trees all around me. I twisted to look down at the ground, almost expecting the darker shadows of Henry and Audra, sliding along, coming back. I knew I wouldn't be able to hear them coming.

TWENTY

Crawling in the tunnel, I pushed my pack ahead until I had to turn back. I could not find a way out, not as quickly as I liked, but I didn't feel like I'd be trapped. I'd left a note behind, too, buried in the blind, in case Audra and Henry returned for me. And even if I was underground when they came back, Henry would be able to find me.

The tunnel slanted down, then up. Smaller tunnels opened in the walls—animal tunnels. I heard the squeak of mice; I thought I put my hand on a snake, slipping away in the darkness. I imagined how soft a fox might be, sliding around me, racing toward the light. I heard scratching and imagined possums, moles, badgers as surprised to find me there as I would be to be so close to them, in that tight space. I remembered a lot of things from *Journey to the Center of the Earth*: the trilobites and the giant gray plants, the mastodon. The dark tunnel floors that felt covered in bones, and the winds, and the way the underground air could suddenly be full of electricity.

The underground winds picked up, they died down. They switched directions, went from warm to cold and from cold to hot. I listened, I thought I heard voices. My dad's voice, just counting numbers. Children singing. Chimes. Audra, crying or laughing. Static. I thought I heard footsteps on the ground above my head. I heard dogs barking, outside, the sound funneled through the tunnel's mouth, echoing around me. The dogs' feet sounded like rain or hail as they ran in a pack across my ceiling.

I felt comfortable, safe down there. When I surfaced, I raised my head very gradually, slowly, into the air, the world. I reached out and pulled vines and brush toward me, to cover the tunnel's mouth.

The third day in Forest Park, I lay in the tunnel, beneath the surface where the air was good, underground where no one knew where I was. It was afternoon; I could smell and taste the dirt beneath the leaves where I rested my head. I must have fallen asleep—I woke up and I couldn't tell what time it was because of the way the light filtered down, and the sound of birds singing. I sat up, put on my shoes, shook the dirt from my hair. Slowly, carefully I raised my head up inside the tree branch I'd dragged across the tunnel's mouth. That way I was still hidden, and I could look in every direction. Trees and snags and bushes, all overgrown.

I pushed the branch aside, stretched my arms above my head. It felt good to stand up straight.

"Vivian. Do you even know how dirty you are?"

I turned around—the voice didn't sound right, not like Audra's, and it took a moment to see where it was coming from.

Taffy stood ten feet away, smiling at me.

"I didn't hear you," I said. "I mean, I didn't know where you were."

"I know," she said. "I've been following you. I know what you do."

I climbed out of the hole, sat down, and unzipped

my pack. As I drank from my water bottle I felt her come closer, her shadow on me.

"You don't know what I do," I said.

I felt her hand touch my water bottle, and I let her take it, watched as she drank, water spilling in white lines down her neck, alongside the long white scar that cut down from behind her ear. She had a scab on her fore-head and her dark hair was much longer on one side, full of knots. Her shoes didn't match. One blue sneaker, one white one. On the white one it said TAF in black marker.

"I saw the posters with you on them." She sat down next to me, close, our knees almost touching. "Your picture and your name, and your sister's picture and her name. Your hair was longer and you looked different, but still I knew it was you."

I took out a hard, round rice cake from my pack and took a bite. When she reached out, I handed it to her and got another for myself. It made me feel good to know there were posters, that Mom and Dad had made them.

"How far does that scar go," I said, "under your shirt?"

"You want to see?"

"No," I said.

"Far," she said.

I looked across the little clearing where a yellow rho-
dodendron was starting to bloom.

"I thought you didn't really have parents," she said.
"I thought you were like me, but then I saw that poster."

"Everyone has parents," I said.

"But yours are looking for you. You could go back
there and live with them, even without your sister."

"She's coming for me," I said.

"What did your parents do to you?" Taffy said.

"Nothing." I twisted the lid back onto my water bottle.

Taffy leaned forward, then, and pulled up the back of
her shirt. Scars showed white against her pale skin, knots
that were raised just a little. Reaching out, I touched her
skin, rested my hand there. I was afraid, for a moment,
that I'd take hold of her and not let go, that I'd scare her,
but then I was able to pull my hand back to myself, to
rest it in my lap.

"They're on my legs, too," she said.

"From the electricity?"

"Some," she said. "But mostly from my foster parents, back in Spokane."

The sound of her voice made me think she might be crying, so I leaned forward, to see her face. She was staring straight ahead, her expression serious, but she wasn't crying. She pulled her shirt back down, over her scars.

"This is an okay place to stay for a little while," she said, "but not for a long time, not really a place to live."

"People do live here," I said. "A girl lived here with her dad for four years."

Taffy laughed. She took a stick in her hand like a sword and started tapping on every stone that she could reach.

"They got caught," she said. "I knew her, that girl. We were locked up at the same police station, after that time they caught her. And then I saw her again, later, with her father on the street. They were running away."

"You didn't really know her," I said.

"Her name was Caroline," Taffy said. "She wasn't really that nice."

"Maybe she was just shy," I said.

"Maybe. They even tried to come back here to live, but that didn't work. They didn't fit."

"Where did they go?"

"Somewhere. Anyway, I'm just saying this isn't an easy place to stay."

"I can wait," I said. "I can live here until my sister comes back for me."

"Your sister?" Taffy looked away, into the trees, back again. "Your sister, I don't think she's coming back here."

"She is," I said. "You don't know."

"It's Henry," she said. "He left town, like last week or something."

"Who told you that?"

"Everyone knows that."

"And Audra?" I said.

"She must have gone, too. Haven't heard of her being around."

"What else haven't you told me?" My voice was rising.

"Don't be mad," Taffy said. "I was afraid you'd get mad, and I wanted you to like me, and I didn't want you to leave."

"You should have told me," I said.

"Let go of me," she said.

"I'm sorry." I let go of her arm; I hadn't realized I'd taken hold of it.

In the silence, I looked down at my feet, dangling in the black hole of the tunnel.

"Where are you sleeping tonight?" Taffy said.

"I don't know," I said.

"In the ground, or in your hammock, or where?"

"That's later," I said.

"Can I stay with you?" she said. "Can I sleep where you sleep?"

"I don't know."

"Are you still mad?" she said. "Don't be."

"It's not that," I said.

We sat there in the silence for a little while, the shadows stretching toward us, and then Taffy got up and walked away. I almost said something, went after her—I wanted her to stay with me, so I would not be alone, so lonely, but then I knew it would be complicated to explain when Henry and Audra came back for me. They'd always wanted me to be so careful, not to talk to anyone else.

I sat there and watched Taffy go into the trees until I couldn't see her anymore.

TWENTY-ONE

Dusk is an uncomfortable time, the way the light is. I crossed the tree line, off the fire road and through a thick meadow, then back into the shadows. It's not easy to see everything right, and it's the most likely time to be surprised. I read about this in the books; I was aware.

I climbed up into the tree house and lay there on my stomach, running my fingertips along the letters I'd carved, listening to the wind in the trees all around me. Out in the meadow, black against the moonlight, crows were arguing, tearing open a plastic bag they'd found. I watched, curious what was inside, and then there was something else, someone coming through the forest.

At first I thought she was a drunk person. She didn't really look like a girl at first, just a person stumbling along, bouncing against tree trunks, tripping into bushes and snarls of blackberries. She passed right beneath me, her hands out in front of her, her head jerking from side to side, and that's when I knew it was Audra.

"Wait!" I said. "It's me."

She didn't slow, and I tried to keep her in sight as I climbed and slid down out of the tree. I had to chase after her, to get around in front of her to get her to stop, and even then she didn't recognize me right away.

"Audra," I said.

She looked past me. Her hair was all wet, sticking out one side, and her face was dirty and scratched, dried blood on her forehead, on her chin. Her neck was black. She wore camouflage pants and a torn T-shirt, laces trailing from her boots. All of her clothes were dripping wet, and it was not raining at all, it hadn't been raining.

I tried to slow her down and she slapped my hands away. The sound of our hands, or the feeling of my skin, finally made her slow, made her notice me.

"Where are our things?" she said. "I hid them all, I put them someplace."

"The blind's over there," I said. "I'll help you. Slow down."

"If I can find them, then I can meet Vivian there, I can find her and tell her—"

"But I'm here," I said. "It's me. Right here. You found me. I found you."

I led her along. I wanted to get her to the first aid kit. I stayed close in case she fell or she tried to run away. The darkness was suddenly thick all around us.

"Where's Henry?" I said. "What happened?"

She started rushing again, then her boot fell off and she stumbled.

"I don't know." She suddenly looked at me, at my face. "Vivian! It's you."

"Yes," I said.

"I'm sorry," she said. "I'm sorry. It was me. I was afraid he was going to choose you, that you'd both leave me."

"I would never," I said.

"I didn't know!"

"Slow down," I said.

"It's too late," she said. "It's impossible. It's too late for that."

"No," I said. "What? What happened?"

"The boat in the water," she said, "and the capsizing—"

"Where?"

"We flipped over, into the cold water, the depths is where I'm coming from, to you—"

Her voice stuttered, her words got louder and quieter like she couldn't control them.

"Vivian!" she said. "You need to think about what to do, where to go. I can't figure out what is the right thing and I've already made mistakes."

"You're coming with me," I said. "We'll find him. We can still go."

Audra made a sound like the beginning of a kind of laugh in her throat.

"No," she said. "I can't. It's too late for that, it's way too late, and even coming here now, tonight, is impossible. I don't know if it can ever happen again."

"Why?" I said. "What are you saying? I'll stay with you."

"Vivian," she said. "You have to listen. I came back so you would know that I'm sorry. I made a mistake! We capsized, Vivian."

We crossed a meadow, our shadows sliding in the tall grass. Audra's hands were dark, almost black under the moon, like they'd been burned. I don't know if she could feel that I held on to her shirt as we walked.

"You kept a secret," she said. "You kept a secret from me."

"What?" I said.

"About the notebook, the writings in there—"

"They were for me," I said. "You wouldn't have believed me. You left me."

When we got to the blind, she didn't want me to touch her, wouldn't let me clean her cuts and scratches. The Band-Aids wouldn't stick, like water was coming out of her body, and she didn't want the headlamp on at all.

All she wanted was to lie down next to me, to be beside me. I wrapped her in the blanket, I tried to dry her off with my clothes. The wetness kept coming through.

"You're not leaving me again," I said.

"I'm hardly even here," she said.

"You are here."

"I'm here and I'm not here."

"Where's Henry?" I said.

"I don't know that," she said. "I lost track, I haven't seen him. He's not here, he's not there."

"Calm down," I said. "Slow down."

"There's no time!" she said. "I'm sorry. I came back because I miss you so much and I always want to take care of you but I can't take care of you, now. I want you to know that, to trust yourself, to remember me."

"Audra," I said. "You're here."

There was the wind in the trees, an owl calling. A dog barked, far away. Audra rolled over, her eyes catching the light.

"I waited," I said. "I found a tunnel, but I didn't find anyone in it. Did you see me? Did you watch me? I missed you when you were gone but I knew you'd come back for me."

"It can be so upside down," Audra said, her whisper breaking into a shout, then going quiet again. "The nets spill out on the deck and the fish are silver in the sun. From the bottom of the ocean you can see the dark triangles way up high, boats sliding on your ceiling. You can't breathe but it doesn't hurt and the salmon are like birds flying smooth around you without a sound, the nets like a cloud coming through."

"Audra," I said. "What are you talking about?"

"The bottom of the ocean," she said.

It was quiet for a while. Audra's breathing sounded raspy, and I wondered if she'd fallen asleep. She smelled like metal, in that tight space, like salt.

"Where I am now," she said. "I can understand better how you are, everything that comes rushing at you, Vivian, the voices—"

"What?"

"But I don't understand it all yet and I don't know what will happen. There's still so much for you to do. I don't have the words but I will, I'll send them—"

"How?" I said. "Quiet."

"I didn't understand before, I couldn't," she said. "I wanted to take care of, protect you."

"It's all right," I said. "We'll be all right."

"A current underwater is just like a wind in the sky,"

she said. "Only thicker. A body can roll along the bottom for miles and miles until it simply comes apart."

"You'll stay with me," I said.

"It's impossible. It's too late for that. But I am with you always."

She sat up and crawled out of the blind—so suddenly and I was after her, so fast the blind came apart on top of me. I shook it off and I was out in the darkness where it was impossible to see. I could only hear Audra stumbling around in the night.

"Don't forget me," she called, suddenly farther away. "Don't forget that I love you, Vivian."

And then there were only the black tree trunks, there was only the night.

TWENTY-TWO

The next morning, the forest was quiet. I'd
rebuilt the blind in the night, before I finally fell asleep. I
slept there, in case Audra came back, even though I knew,
I could feel, that she wasn't coming back.

I carried my pack, my shoes, in my hands. I wandered
through the forest, crawled through the tunnels, climbed
into the tree house. I watched the birds, the boats and
bridges, the river below. I thought I would find Taffy, I
hoped she would find me, but I did not and she did not.

I walked down into the city in the afternoon. At Pioneer Square, I bought a burrito from a cart and sat on the
steps for an hour, trying to figure out what to do. Around

me, street kids were kicking a hacky-sack. Skateboards were off to one side, with some dogs and girls. I'm sure Taffy knew them, and they knew her, but she wasn't there. Audra probably knew some of those kids, too, and maybe even some of them recognized me, but that didn't matter. I wasn't going to join them, didn't want to stay outside any longer on my own.

Audra had said there was a lot for me to do, and that was how I felt, but I didn't even know how to begin, how to continue. I knew that I wanted to go home, to see my parents, to wait there, even if I'd only have to leave again.

It wasn't until dusk that I decided this, that I caught the train, rode across the river, back to our neighborhood.

Nothing felt like I knew it and still I kept on, slowly and quietly. The moon was full, and I dragged my black shadow along, past Klickitat Street, right down Siskiyou.

The tire swing was gone. I looked up, saw the raw spot on the tree branch, where the rope had been. And the house seemed darker, painted a color I couldn't quite tell in the moonlight. The footprints from Audra's shoes, above the window, were gone, too. Painted over.

The windows were dark except the one on the side, the kitchen window.

I went around, away from the lit kitchen window, down the driveway. Past the garage, into the backyard. I was crouching low, back in the trees where I could see through the window.

My parents were eating dinner, sitting across from each other, the sides of their faces toward me. They were talking. Something seemed not quite right, and then I realized Dad had shaved off his beard, and cut his hair short. He poured a glass of wine—there was a bottle on the table, next to my mom's pyramid light. She said something to him, glanced away.

I watched them for a little while, maybe to see if I would run away, or if they'd do something that I didn't recognize, that would show me that I shouldn't return. I didn't know what I was going to do until I did it.

At last I crossed the backyard, stood for a moment on the concrete steps. The door was unlocked. I opened it, and stepped inside.

Mom and Dad looked up and didn't move, didn't say anything at first. I set down my pack on the floor, my jacket.

"Vivian."

When Dad stood, his chair fell over backward, bouncing with a crack on the floor. He didn't pick it up. It seemed like he wanted to step closer to me but didn't want to scare me away.

"Are you hungry, honey?" Mom said.

"Yes," I said.

I ate three bowls of chili, sitting between them, and drank two glasses of milk. They watched me eat. They didn't say anything. Mom switched off her pyramid light and they just watched me, careful and tentative like I might suddenly stand up and bolt for the door, disappear again.

I didn't look straight at them, but I liked having their faces there, at the edge of my vision. I could imagine someone watching me, from out in the trees. I liked being in the warm kitchen again, the feeling of the fork in my hand, the sound of the refrigerator. I could see through the doorway, into the living room, where a new television rested on a stand.

"And Audra?" Mom said, her voice soft.

"I'm back," I said. "I'm really here."

"Where is she now?"

"It's too late for her," I said.

"Can't you tell us something?"

Standing up, I wiped my mouth. "She's never coming back."

"Stay," Dad said. "You don't have to tell us everything right away. Wait."

"All I want," I said, "all I want is to take a shower and then to sleep in my bed."

TWENTY-THREE

I slept almost until noon in my clean sheets,
and when I woke up I could hear Mom and Dad, downstairs in the kitchen. I couldn't tell what they were saying, but I liked the sound of their voices, mixed with the
rain on the rooftop.

I lay there like that, listening, and then I got up and
walked across the hall into Audra's room. It was just like
the last time I'd seen it, and it still smelled like paint. The
blue walls, the empty shelves. I sat down on her bed.

There were footsteps on the stairs, and then Mom
stood in the doorway, watching me. I didn't look up,
but she came in and sat down on the bed, too. She put
her hand on my shoulder for a moment and set it down

on her lap again. There was only the sound of the rain.

After a little while, I could tell that she was crying.

"Are you going to work?" I said.

"No," she said. "We'll stay home until we're sure you're okay. We'll need to get straight with school and the doctor and everything—"

"School?" I said.

"Not until you're ready," she said. "Mostly we want to make sure you're all right."

"I am," I said. "I think I am. And I don't need the doctor. I'm fine."

"Just a checkup."

"I'm not taking the pills anymore," I said.

"We'll see," she said.

Around us, the blue walls looked perfectly smooth. The drawers of the desk were closed, and the door of Audra's closet.

"You changed everything in this room," I said. "All her things."

Out the window, the tree's wet leaves shone.

"We got your letter," she said. "You said you were with Audra—"

"That was before," I said.

"You said you were moving away. Where were you?"

"I can't—" I said. "I can't tell you that, about that, yet." My fingers were itching, and my hands felt like they were about to start shaking.

"It's all right." Mom touched me again, then stood up. "It's all right. It is. Are you hungry? Why don't you get dressed, then come down and have something to eat?"

"Sit down," I said.

"What?"

"Just sit beside me for a little bit," I said. "Sit with me. We don't have to talk."

Mom sat down again and I could feel that she was close and smell her perfume, hear her breath. It was tender, and we stayed like that until Dad called up, saying he was making lunch.

When I went downstairs I put my shoes back on and walked outside, into the backyard. The rain had stopped, and I crossed the wet grass. I checked that my bike was still in the garage, and then I walked out to the edge of the yard, under the trees. I looked up into the empty branches where Henry had once hidden, that first night

I met him, when he came for me. I could feel Mom and Dad watching me from the house, their nervousness, even if I couldn't see them in the windows.

It was later on that first day after my return that I was drinking orange juice in the kitchen and heard Dad in the basement. There was the creak of his chair, the switching of switches.

He didn't notice me, at first, coming down the stairs, standing behind him. I pulled over a wooden chair, from next to the washing machine, and sat down next to him. Then he smiled, pulled the headset down, around his neck.

"You shaved your beard," I said.

"I did."

"Why?"

"I missed you," he said. "I really missed you a lot. I was just telling some friends that you came back." He reached his arm loosely around the back of my chair, then, and I could smell the dusty smell of his wool shirt that I liked, and could see the skin of his head through the tangle of his hair.

"My girl," he said.

Sounds, words, buzzed in the round black earpieces

around his neck. In the lighted glass windows, the red needles jerked.

"I missed you, too," I said, and before it got quiet I said, "You have a friend in Iceland?"

"Did I tell you that?"

"Yes. Is that her name?"

"I doubt it." He laughed, scratched the side of his face. "That's what she calls herself, though, and from her call sign I can tell that's where she is. The numbers tell me."

"And what else?"

"About her?" he said. "You know, mostly we talk about the weather, or she asks me about you girls. She has two sons—she's very old, and they want to put her in an old folks' home, but she has some kind of a truck, with a radio setup, and she drives around from place to place like that."

"In a truck, in Iceland?"

"That's what she told me."

Dad wore those ragged felt boot liners, and sitting close to him it smelled like his wool shirt, and coffee. His dented thermos sat on the desk, his blue mug next to his logbook.

"Whatever happens in our family," he said, "that's for us to figure out, to try to understand. We'll work it out the best way we can. It hasn't been easy for your mom, for any of us."

It was quiet, then, and I wondered which one of us would stand up first, climb the stairs to the kitchen.

"How did you meet her?" I said.

"Your mom?" he said. "You know that story."

"No," I said, "this other lady. Iceland."

"Oh, that was a couple of years ago. I was just listening in, on different channels, and I heard her talking about Number Stations, and that was interesting, she sounded interesting."

"Why?"

"Here." He pulled the headset from his neck and closed it down to make it smaller before putting it over my head, the black foam around my ears so I heard the sound of the ocean, my blood circling. And then he switched the switch and turned the dial. In the middle of the tiny window, the red needle lifted.

I heard a tone, a beeping like someone tapping the key of an electrical organ as fast as they could, then someone whispering, then a woman counting in a language I didn't know. Dad reached out, switched the station, turned the dial. In my ears another woman said, "Mike, India, Whiskey, One, Delta, Four, Seven, Delta." Static crowded around the voice, and she was serious like she was reading the numbers, trying to be sure that she got the numbers right, that she didn't get lost. "I say, Three, Two, Eight, Delta," and then a buzzing, a machine behind her. The hairs came up on my arms, a chill inside, a kind of feeling that was like seeing something at night and not knowing what it is, or when a dog barks at you and you don't know if it's going to bite or lick your hand. I couldn't tell what it was. Dad turned the dials again, to another number, and then there was the woman again, speaking more quickly, sounding scared: "Nancy, Adam, Susan, Nancy, Adam, Susan."

Dad watched me, listening. He switched off the radio and helped me take the headset off my ears.

"What was that?" I said.

"Just messages that were sent out."

"Who sends them?" I said.

"No one knows," he said. "They're a kind of code,

and they play at the same time every day, or some never stop. Some people think they're for spying, for spies and their secrets."

"But Iceland understands them," I said.

"Oh, no," he said. "I don't think so. She just thinks they're beautiful."

He told me how the sounds and numbers and words stood in for letters, and that only two people had the code to make sense of the message. The sender, and the receiver. He showed me the chart on the wall, all the frequencies where the Number Stations were found. I put the headset back on and listened as he turned the dial. Static, and then a bugle. Buzzers speeding up, music playing too slow or fast or backward, the sound of a gong, and always people counting, men and women and children in different languages, in different orders, circling and circling around. They sent out their message for years and years, hoping that someone would understand them, that they would find the right person.

TWENTY-FOUR

Today I'm going to finish writing this. That doesn't mean the story is over, or that there aren't other stories. I've written to the end of the blue notebook, then a green one, then red, and now into another blue one. I wanted to show what happened to my sister, and how I got from where I was to where I am. That's what it means to finish this.

The yellow notebook, the words slowed, but they haven't stopped. New words rose up in it, not long after I came home:

> *One single bolt or screw holds a scissors*
> *together. Animals quickly take notice of*

white teeth and the whites of the eyes.
We can read the animals, and you pick
up on things others don't. Hello, we are
interested in you. Klickitat. Our bodies are
so fluid, they can hardly be called bodies,
they are made for where we are. The words
and sentences we say still wait in the air;
words find their channels, traveling in
currents like at the bottom of the oceans,
a channel cut to depths where the signals
can find you. Hello, it's your sister and
I am coming apart as I write you from
beyond. We will tell you the when and
the where, the what to do, but we must be
patient, all of us. We wait, always moving,
never still, for the time. The time must be
ripe, right—not rife, that is a different
word, a disagreement. A disagreement
changes the air in a room for a time. Every
word means something different to every
person. We think we understand what
someone is saying, but we don't, not really.

Sometimes we make sense and sometimes
we make no sense. I'm sorry and a current
underwater is a wind in the sky, we can
breathe, but it doesn't hurt. We are your
sister and more than your sister. The words
and sentences we say still wait in the air,
even after the sound is gone, hoping some-
one will come along and understand them.
And words that we write down or read, too,
are messages that we send out again and
again, trying to find the right person, the
person who will understand.

Some of this seemed familiar to me; reading back
through the yellow notebook, I recognized sentences
from earlier messages, all shuffled together, mixed with
new sentences, other voices. I remembered things Henry
had said to me, and Audra. I thought about the books
I'd been reading. The words came snarled, all at once.
Sounding me, seeking a channel.

TWENTY-FIVE

I keep expecting Audra's voice, or her foot-steps clattering up the stairs. Mom and Dad never raise their voices, never make any loud noises; they are so careful, almost afraid of me. They tell me things will get easier, and they will, they do. And then, at the same time, I don't feel that I belong here, that I will stay.

I have written this sincerely. I never asked for any-thing to change, to see and hear beyond this world around me. That's one way to say it: In one of Audra's books, *Indians of the American Northwest*, I read that Klick-itat is not just the street in my neighborhood, the street where Beezus and Ramona live in the books, and it is not only the name of a county in Washington and a river. It is also the name of an Indian tribe. The Indian word *Klickitat* means "beyond."

I was back for two weeks before Mom and Dad would leave me by myself at home. Even after they went to work, I kept expecting them to double back, to check on me. Mom called me five times and Dad four, that first day, to know that I was home, and I could tell by the sounds around them that they were at work. That meant that I had some time before they could make it home, if they decided to come check on me.

What I did, then, was go downstairs and switch on my dad's radio. I sat down in his chair, put the earpieces of the headset over my ears, and dialed in the numbers.

"CQ, TF8GX," I said into the microphone. "N7NTU calling TF8GX. CQ."

I could hear my breathing inside my head, and then bursts of static, the voice finally rising through it, becoming clearer and louder.

"Be happy," she said.

"Iceland," I said.

"You wandered your way back home—your father told me so. He must be so happy. He's been so worried. And your sister?"

"She's gone," I said.

"You're there," Iceland said. "I'm here. Let's have a conversation."

"Okay," I said.

"I like to talk to people who can't see me," Iceland said. "Though my walking is improving, day by day. When I was a girl, I couldn't walk at all. I just sat in my wheelchair all day watching the barges go by—did I tell you that?"

"Yes," I said. "Are you really in a truck?"

"In the back of a truck," she said. "It's a camper, of a sort. With an antenna, yes, and windows and this radio setup. I can see the lava flows now, out my window."

"You like the Number Stations," I said. "My dad told me that. You listen to them."

"Yes," Iceland said. "That is correct."

"I listened," I said. "I don't know how it made me feel."

"They're mysterious," she said, "those stations, and

sometimes they make me sad, sometimes they make me hopeful. It's nice and it's sad, isn't it, to think that they're always out there, waiting for someone to understand them?"

"But you don't understand them," I said.

"Me? No, not really, I don't."

"Spies use them," I said. "That's what Dad said."

"Spies?" she said. "That's what he said?"

"Are you a spy?"

"I wouldn't say so. I believe I'd know if I were."

The static rose up in my ears, a thick tangle, and I didn't know how to change that, and for a moment I thought our talk was over.

"People are always trying to reach people," she said. "Sometimes people who aren't alive anymore."

"But you're alive," I said.

"Of course I am. I'm old, but I'm still here! But the others, they can sound so different. My sister Berglind, for instance—she talks in the voice she had as a little girl."

"What does she say?"

"She says that she loves me, and that it's crowded, that the winds blow every direction where she is. Still, she speaks to me, her little voice finds a way through the static."

"I get messages in a notebook," I said, after a moment. "Handwriting."

"They can come to us any number of ways," she said.

"It's from a lot of people at once," I said. "So it's hard to understand."

"Of course it is," Iceland said.

Again, the static—voices whispering, pieces of words. Again, it cleared.

"I'm listening for my sister," she said. "My sister Berglind, who has died. She comes on different channels, she's trying to find me. Dead people have to learn to talk again, how to count, how to make any kind of sense. And we also need to be patient, to listen."

"I'm patient," I said. "I can be."

"How did you lose your sister?" Iceland said.

I'd been watching the red needle as it lifted and fell, as it jerked with our words, but now that was blurry, the tears in my eyes. I closed my eyes and all I could see was the black of Audra's neck, all I could hear was what she said about the body rolling across the bottom of the ocean.

"She drowned," I said. "She was in a boat and it capsized."

"And that's where she is now?"

"I think so." I was crying. I held my hand over the microphone.

"You can still talk with her," Iceland said. "It will take time. Everything you need to know is inside you, the same as it's inside her. You'll figure out how to talk to each other. You'll have to figure out how to listen, to understand."

"I'm listening," I said. "I will."

"It's so cold, here," she said. "I can see snow on the volcanoes, right from this window."

"Volcanoes?" I said.

"You're thinking of Snæfell, yes? The one from the book?"

The static again, my curled toes cold inside my socks.

"Is it cold there?" she said.

"Not really," I said. "It might still be raining."

"There is so much for you to do," she said. "So many places."

"How do you know?" I said.

"I can feel it," she said. "Let's have another conversation, another time."

TWENTY-SIX

Yesterday I walked in Forest Park. The sun was out—it's almost summer, now. It wasn't easy to find where the blind had been, but I found it. All torn apart, the box dug up and stolen.

I climbed up into the tree house and read the letters I cut into the wood. **KLICKITAT**. There was no answer carved there.

The only tunnel I saw was when a rabbit shot across the path, disappeared into its hole.

I saw people, but not Taffy, not Audra, not Henry.

I still think about Henry. I wonder. Did he make it back to where he was from? Did he also drown? Will he write to me? I wait, I listen. At night I think about how he can see in the dark and I remember his deep voice, the way he walked, all the stretches and yoga poses, the things he'd do with his body. His feet and hands, the sound of him cracking his knuckles. He appreciated me, the ways I am different. Will he come back for me? When will the messages tell me where and how to find him?

We will tell you the when and the where, the what to do, and still we must be patient, all of us.

Henry needs me, he said that, like he said his people needed the man who could hear the boats coming by listening to the ground, who could read animals and see people others couldn't see. *Klickitat* is a word that means beyond, different than how this world is, around me, and when Henry comes I'll be ready to go with him.

Klickitat. Audra, she is watching me, listening. I miss her, and I feel that she is here, as much as she can be.

My hair has grown, but the last few inches are still black, reminding me of that time when we were last together. I'm stronger now, I don't take any pills, I stay hopeful. Sometimes I feel I'm writing to her, and other times it might be for people I don't even know. It keeps the agitation away, it keeps me balanced, it keeps me safe.

I used to be so snarled up inside, agitated, all these waves and words tangled on each other with no place to go, a pressure that kept building and building. Now my snarl is sounds, voices, words.

Here in the notebooks I've let it out, I've collected all these different words. The ones in the yellow notebook, they found me, they find me still. They are the words that came from beyond, because I was ready to receive them. And then the rest of the words, these words I'm writing now—they don't feel so different, they also come through me. I listen in; I intercept them. I receive these words and send them out again, so they can reach the next person.